The Golden Gate Is Red

The Golden Gate Is Red

Jim Kohlberg

OPEN ROAD

INTEGRATED MEDIA

NEW YORK

This dedication, a long time in coming, falls upon the strong shoulders of my mother and father.

Until that spring in San Francisco, I did not fuck with death and it did not fuck with me. Until then, mistakes could be rectified, regrets consumed by time, and kidnapped love recaptured. Until that March, I knew not death and it knew not me.

But now it fills my heart and hands and nose, like the smell of the rich California loam I threw on Joe's coffin, the dry peaty warmth of the clods thudding on the cherrywood, the dust of it staining my palms.

We're born dying and we know it—that's what I found that spring of 2003. I carry it with me every waking day.

Chapter 1

The first Tuesday in March, Christina's letter landed on my desk. March 4 was the kind of day San Franciscans smugly live for, bright and clear and dry. From my converted office in North Beach on the back side of Telegraph Hill, I could see the streets below were relatively empty, post-dotcom-crash traffic had thinned out, and parking was mercifully and shockingly available. The Gods of Ease had smiled upon the city just as the Titans of Commerce had deserted it.

Christina and I had North Beach the way expats had Paris, full of pleasure and life. Our North Beach was the North Beach of Café Rico—family platters of garlic-stuffed veal and plates mounded with fusilli and bowls of grilled shrimp—of long coffee mornings and late night, wine-soaked walks down Broadway, giggling at the bunch of bordellos and theaters. North Beach was an innocent Paris, a pre-dotcom quiet that even now after the crash has never returned, if it was ever there at all. I should have been grateful to Christina for that brief and eternal city of love, but it's always hard to feel grateful to someone who amputates a thigh without benefit of anesthesia. No, it's hard to be grateful for that.

Standing outside my office door, I watched two jays squawk and jabber from branch to branch. The new buds on the branches were that delicate shade of green that reminds me of young children. The still bare limbs the jays clung to recalled winter not long past.

Inside, my assistant, Irene, was waiting for me, hands on her nonexistent hips, a farmhouse print dress sharply at odds with the blackbird eyes, jerky and annoyed, perched above too-bright red lips. Once, when I mentioned the thickness of her makeup, she pointedly added to it. Since then I've acquired enough wisdom, without the benefit of marriage, to keep my mouth shut. She stabbed the letter at me before I even crossed the threshold.

"Open this," she demanded.

I looked down at the white corner, almost touching my breastbone, ready to eviscerate my upper ribs. There was a little tremor to the envelope as Irene's fingers twisted with indignation or anger and God only knows what else. I stalled for time.

"Mind if I have a cup of coffee first?" I asked.

"It's personal and confidential," she said, "so I didn't touch it."

"Thank you."

"You know how I hate those. There's no reason I can't open them."

"No. There's no reason, Irene. I really don't need privacy. I don't need to have one or two things that you don't know about, a little tiny part of me you don't get to see. Not any bigger than this envelope," I said, reaching out for the envelope and pulling it from her three fingers.

Irene and I had long ago settled into our domesticated habits; she learned about all my peccadilloes and miscues, then explained each as the fault of grasping harpies or the product of envious lies. She had written off men long ago, on the heels of a scattering husband who left her with a car hocked to its eyeballs and three months of back rent. A wayward uncle had materialized soon after, and she had taken him in like a stray cat, turning him into a decent househusband while she stayed in the world as the breadwinner.

"It smells," she said, her nose wrinkled in derision, nodding at the envelope disappearing into my overstuffed briefcase—the handles already stretched so that my fingers had become as strong as a tennis pro's from lugging it around.

"Of perfume," she added.

"Oh," I said, putting the bulging sack down and taking up the letter again. I was a shade embarrassed to sniff the envelope in front of her, and it hovered again in approximately the same position she had pointed it at me.

"There's only one person who sends scented letters," she said.

This allowed me to put it to my face. Sure enough, the spicy earthy tones of Christina, strongest behind her small ears where she dabbed it with a pinky. The place where senses defeated caution. A scent unnamed and undivulged. No matter how many times I had asked.

I looked at the writing. It looked like her hand, though there was a spikiness to this script that made me doubt it until I saw our familiar joke as the address: Max Smoller, Tax Detective. My address was scrawled on the front, but there was no return name on the back, just an apartment number and street. Typical of

Christina's misbegotten and quixotic notion of privacy: never a correct name but a perfectly valid address, waiting for some Internet pirate or simply a detective who could walk. I turned my eyes on Irene, looking up at her with as hard a look as I could manufacture.

"So what?" I shrugged.

"Don't you let that hussy near you again."

"She's married, Irene," I said.

"I think we both know that."

"It's just a letter, for God's sake."

"A scented letter," she said, turning to stomp up the stairs in her plastic clogs and black socks. Her white freckled face had a flush of red, protective anger to it, and the black pageboy whipped around as she turned away. I read disgust in the hunched curve of her shoulders.

I climbed the two short flights into the renovated octagonal tower that was my office. I had bought the building, a bankrupt restaurant, for the panoramic views of San Francisco and its bejeweled bay. The floor below my office, now the conference room, had been my ex-partner Joe's office. Joe the shooting star. Pass the bar without law school Joe. Joe who was never going to last as a forensic tax accountant, slowly spinning his life away over the dry, dusty tax returns of wealthy patrons who weren't smart enough or honest enough to pay their taxes and then called us in to rescue them when the government bloodhounds picked up their trails. That Joe.

And bloodthirsty hounds they were. If you think hell hath no fury like a woman scorned, you should meet IRS agents when they get the pungent whiff of fraud on a tax return that should be coughing up millions while they're making fifty or sixty thousand a year and driving home to the split-level in a twelve-year-old Taurus. They live for cases like that.

Joe Dempsey was never going to stay in practice with me, battling vengeful or envious agents. He knew that he was meant for bigger things. Some of us know our destiny and have the strength to reach for it. Others are so sure of it that they don't even have to try; it shines on them like moonbeams and pixie dust. Joe was one of those. It just so happens that when he left me on his moonbeam, he took Christina with him while I watched them disappear, chained to earth, bound to an empty North Beach where I walked with memories and ghosts.

I tapped the letter against my jeans, telling myself I wouldn't open it—that I had the strength not to. The kind Irene thought I had. In front of me I could see the sun bounce off the deep red of the Golden Gate's painted steel. That was San Francisco's first big lie. Mine was, I would leave that letter alone.

I took a knife and attacked the edge of the envelope. I might as well rip the Band-Aid off the wound. Christina's aroma wafted out as I pulled the note free and laid it on my table desk.

"Dear Max," it read, though I heard the musical but deep-throated voice in my ears as I silently read the words:

I trust and pray this letter finds you well. I have often heard of your growing reputation for saving those who have much and are unable to part with it, even under the unbending eyes of the IRS.

I must ask you for help, despite my anticipation that you will refuse. I plead in the name of the rare joy that was ours years ago. Please, Max. I need you.

Forever yours,
Christina

Forever Yours, right. More like Never Yours. It seemed the rest of the world, or at least Joe and Christina, had the gift of reimagining memory to suit them. I missed that survival course.

I sat back in my Aeron chair, leaned my head back, and twisted left to watch cars snaking out the Waldo Tunnel on the Sausalito side of the bay, approaching through the square buttresses and wide highway leading to the Golden Gate Bridge. Underneath the span, wind whipped the currents to a white-capped, spraying frenzy, throwing off shafts of blue, green, and gray mist in the gleaming morning sun. Mist and fog hovered beyond the gate, out over the ocean, and the rust-colored bridge spans soaked up the sun as the flock of shiny cars passed under them.

With a harsh closure and constriction burning in my throat, I dropped the letter, a flush crawling up my face. It was ridiculous and it was typical. It was pleading and demanding and manipulative all at the same time; the elegant English accent came through the page, a tiny, subtle or imagined break here and there betraying her Des Moines origins: the unembarrassed, imperious plea, white handkerchief wrung over tears, eyelashes batting. No apology, no admission, just the assumption that it was all fond memories and I was over her. She was right about that. Damn right.

She had made one mistake, though. She had not come in person. It was hard to describe, really, her presence. Beauty doesn't begin to announce such a heart attack, if only because she wasn't exquisite. Her features were off-kilter and slightly out of place. Lovely curves, great legs, round ass, and fulsome breasts, oh yes. But none of these describe her fully.

Perhaps it was just the whiteness of her teeth, the satin white she was continually checking in every shiny surface, or the green eyes—mercurial, changeable, shade-able, blue-able—framed by her winter wheat hair; but when she turned to you, putting a touch of light cool fingertips on your arm and focusing the smile and eyes on you . . . well, you thought you both were all alone on earth. Alone with ancients and gods. She somehow opened all the unfilled holes that remain closed. Those deep, mildewed wells we all rein in and cover with our straight and heavy man-holes, those dark places opened to the light of her smile with the immediate presumption that she would fill them. Fill them with her blinding . . . what? A siren as old as man himself, as unhinged, and as irresistible.

Yes, I could say she had made a mistake in not coming.

"Irene," I barked.

"You don't have to yell. I'm right here," she said, suddenly materializing in the door of my office.

"I wasn't yelling."

"Your ears must be farther from your mouth than mine," she said.

"Take a letter," I said.

Eyebrows. Irene's eyebrows were her most potent weapon. And now they were climbing spaceward like military jets over Crissy Field.

"Your computer broken?" she asked.

"What do you do around here?" I asked.

"Filing, phones, mail, half of all the returns you look at, which means you bill me out at $250 per hour and pay me at what? Less than $100," she said, hands on hips now. "Anything else I forgot?"

"Yeah, back talk," I answered. "But you'll like this. So sit still a minute and write, please."

She managed to lean against my desk and prop a pen and small pad in her hand.

7

Dear Christina,

Good to hear from you after all this time. I hope you and Joe are well.

Anyway, I am afraid I can't really help now. I am very busy. Call Arthur Knopp at Rayburn and Marberry. He's very competent. Very understanding. Joe knows him.

Best,

Max

"Well. I do like that," Irene said. "I'll dig around for a current address. Seems you've finally gotten her out of your system?"

"Long ago."

"I thought that endless procession of petite bottle blondes was simply revenge," she said.

"I like blondes. And anyway, I'm dating a brunette," I said. "Or I was until a few days ago."

"What happened?"

"What always happens. Arguments, boredom, expectations. Friendship goes poof."

"You might even be ready for a couple of blind dates," she said.

"With your friends? Not a chance."

"What's wrong with my friends?" she said, putting her hands on her hips again. "They're great women, not girls. Pretty, smart, together. They're just in the wrong city for men. That's all. Otherwise they'd be with someone and you'd be out of luck."

"Nothing's wrong with your friends. They're just your friends."

She shrugged after a bit of searching back into my face. "Suit yourself," she said, closing the notebook over the snarled curlicues of her transcription as she clomped out. Her shorthand wasn't school-taught or readable by anyone else. Which suited me fine.

I turned in my chair to look out at the bay, the climbing sun reducing the morning dazzle to pedestrian brightness. I heard the soft whir of her computer starting up and then a brief staccato clicking of the keyboard. A few minutes later the phone downstairs arrested my assault on a 1040 form. Then my phone jingled and I picked it up.

"Your ten o'clock is here," Irene said.

I hadn't heard the door downstairs open. Usually I heard the small bells on the lintel chime.

"A Mister Cleveland. McClellan Cleveland," she continued.

"McClellan? Is he wearing Confederate gray?"

"Witty," she said.

"Did he hear our little altercation?"

"Fight. Big words don't impress me. We had a fight. And no, he's in the downstairs parlor." And with that, I was dismissed as she hung up.

As I headed downstairs to the ground floor, her shadow moved across the dappled panes of glass between her cubicle and the conference room, then disappeared. I went to what had been the parlor, now conference space, still decorated with the original restaurant's pictures of the city's greater lights—Alioto shaking hands with Herb Caen, a middle-aged Willie Mays hunkered over a beer, and one of Old Man Hearst reading his son's first edition of the Examiner. That one was actually valuable.

I paused at the doorknob. It was time to listen to another client story, why they didn't pay, why they shouldn't. That was, in essence, my job. Create an adaptation, a translation of their story the IRS would buy. I took a breath before going down the rabbit hole of another tale from the economically blessed and ethically impaired.

Chapter 2

I opened the door to the parlor and walked through; Irene had converted it to a small conference room with a round table and coffee credenza.

The man sitting at the table had a sallow face, the color of a beeswax candle. The jaw was long and narrow, ending in a receding chin, the skin flecked with dark stubble and a tiny razor nick. Thin, veined eyelids covered his gray eyes, and a pinched nose with a tip not quite bulbous hung between them. A crown of blond hair had faded and thinned under the man's fifty-odd years. He got up quickly as I entered.

"Mr. Smoller?" he asked, putting out his hand, his left hand. It startled me and I straightened up out of my habitual slouch. I heard my grandmother's Brooklyn whine: "Max, don't shtoop, people will tink you're a schlomock."

"I'm Danny Cleveland," he said while I blinked my grand-mother's voice away and came back to the hum of the air-conditioning. I looked at my right fingertips on the table and almost shoved out the right hand from habit, then slung my left out from where it was hiding behind my hip. I poked it out and he grasped it and moved it up and down a couple of times in a strong bony hand. I left my unfamiliar hand in his until he let it go. I sneaked a look for his right hand, but it was still in his jacket pocket.

"Max Smoller," I said to the gray eyes, filmed with a dullness that didn't match his suit. It was a three-piece, a blue so dark you could wear it to a funeral, with French cuffs and a matching tie clip with cuff links. A white shirt shimmered under the fluores-cents, and a purple tie, the color I saw congressional leaders wear-ing on their photo-op days, splashed purplish light onto his face.

He sat down and put his hands on the table. The right one had a thumb a different shade than the rest of the hand. There was a seam between the base of the thumb and his meaty palm. Both were plastic.

Cleveland kept looking at me, and as I looked up I saw the eyes watch me with wearied amusement, calibrating my reaction with exquisite precision. I sat down across from him, waiting for him to say something about it, feeling the odd sensation of wanting to wiggle my own thumbs. I started to yank my hands into my lap, then moved them more slowly off the table.

"So," I said, to distract him, "what brings you here, Mr. Cleve-land?"

"Danny, if you don't mind."

I looked at the hand on the table. "Danny?" I asked, tilting my head.

He shrugged in a nod. "Joe Dempsey told me about you."

I almost reached to crush his plastic hand, but my hands

remained hidden underneath the table. "Joe Dempsey. That was five years ago." I looked out the window. "Same time of year, March." Another false spring.

"Joe said you were the only one who told him what he didn't want to hear."

I waited a minute trying to figure out whether there was sarcasm underneath. "That's how I make friends and influence people," I said.

Danny Cleveland rolled his plastic hand over and pushed at its palm with his fingertips. The plastic was soft but firm neoprene, and it was discolored and fading away on the back, liver spots gone mad.

He laughed. "Still, Joe said you did a good job for him. At least he could understand what you were saying."

"That's from staying out of law school."

"I thought it came from staying out of prison," Danny Cleveland said, smiling. To show me it was a joke.

I get that a lot now. Accountants and CEOs were suddenly wearing orange and had replaced lawyers and reporters at the bottom of the polls.

"What seems to be your problem?" I asked.

Danny Cleveland said, "I want to kill my IRS auditor." He stopped and looked at me; his dull gray eyes held steadily on a point in the middle of my forehead. I let him do it for a moment. Then I raised my eyebrows. As I was sucking in a breath to speak he cracked a snide white smile.

"Just kidding," he said. "I want you to get the Service to accept my tax returns."

"Everybody does. I'd have to go through your deductions and other . . ."

He interrupted. "You don't understand. I want them to accept my tax payment. They think I am owed a refund."

"A refund."

"Yes."

"And you want to make a tax payment?"

"Actually just not receive the refund."

I gave him my best puzzled-owl look. But it didn't faze him. He still had the same dull gray eyes and the white toothy smile painted on his face.

"Well, that's new," I said.

"Nevertheless."

"You want to pay the Service? More than they are asking?"

"More precisely, I don't want their refund."

"I believe you really do need a lawyer," I said. Then a shrink. Maybe some medication. Pharmaceutical grade.

"I've talked to some. They say there's nothing in the law that requires me getting a refund."

"So get a court order."

"I don't want to raise it to that level. You understand, I'm sure."

"You don't want a refund. You don't want to go to court." I leaned back in my chair and spread my hands. "Avoiding taxes is the national pastime. A tax case has more players than a football team, takes longer than two baseball seasons. But you want to pay more?"

"That's correct."

"That's correct?" I asked. He nodded. "May I ask why?"

His spine stiffened and he came to attention. I was a little sarcastic, I admit.

"I am a patriot, sir."

"A patriot?" I was getting tired of hearing myself parrot every sentence.

"It is a grave time in our country's history. We are at war. Beset by hidden enemies. Are you a student of history, Mr. Smoller?"

"Just the rev procs."

"Pardon?"

"The Service's revenue procedures."

"A pity. You seem bright enough," he said. Get a load of this guy. Eyes that needed Windex to shine them up and he's calling me dim.

"I am a strong supporter of this government. We must find our enemies. They are trying to kill us. We must get them first. Remember, Rome fell because of its own weakness, not its enemy's strength."

"And you want to patriotically overpay your taxes?"

"As I told you. I don't want to collect my refund. At least for now. Perhaps at a later date when our collective danger has passed," he finished.

I let out a sigh. It hung in the empty conference room like smoke that won't blow away. His hands were in his lap, patiently splayed on his thighs, back straight.

"I don't know that there's much I really can do. It really depends on who's got the case."

He smiled. For the first time I saw a little light inside those field-gray eyes.

"I'm offering a hundred thousand dollars. On a success fee basis of course. The chief investigative auditor is critical. Correct?"

I just nodded this time.

"His name is Mr. Redfield," he said, taking a card from his shirt pocket. "Armand Redfield." A loud whistle sounded. The merriment in his eyes was not the end of a tunnel, it was a train. And its name was Senior Auditor Redfield.

"Armand Redfield," I said. "Jesus." I was the one with the dim eyes now. Mr. Cleveland didn't have a response for that one. Armand Redfield and I got along well. Very well—as long as we didn't see each other, talk to each other, or work together. Eight years ago he fired me. "You knew, didn't you?"

"I did," he said, nodding.

"Dempsey?" I asked.

"Joe said you knew Armand well."

"Past tense. And Joe should keep the past in the past."

"Nevertheless," he said, twisting his head to the side.

"Present tense: he hates my guts." I couldn't quite bring myself to tell Danny boy that Armand terminated me from the agency and my certain ascent to secretary of the Treasury.

"Will you take the assignment?"

I bent down and unlocked a drawer on the right side of the credenza using an antique metal key I left in the keyhole. I pulled out a metal box that had been pushed against the back of the drawer, took another key from my jacket, and opened the flimsy lock with a single twist. Inside were stashed a pack of Marlboros and a silver Zippo lighter. I flipped a cigarette out and fired up. I glanced over at Cleveland to see if he would mind. With his good hand he pulled out a pipe and raised his eyebrows in question. I nodded as I sucked in my first puff. Soon the room was blue with smoke.

"All right. I'll give it a try. Give me five thousand now and five when I'm done."

"I'm offering a hundred," said Danny.

"I heard you. This is just going to be a couple of phone calls. I'll let you know how it goes."

He took a pipe tool from his jacket, switched the pipe to his plastic hand, tamped down his bowl, and put it out. He tucked it carefully into his jacket and stood up. Next he took a checkbook from inside his coat and bent over the desk and wrote. He tore the check out and placed it on my desk. By the time I finished my cigarette, he was gone.

Chapter 3

The first week of April floated by. Every spare moment I found myself staring out at white sails on the bay, hungry for blue water and wide sweeps of sun and unchallenged vistas, but I kept wrestling my mind back to the rev procs I needed to research to support Danny Cleveland's tax position. There had to be something hinky about it. He wouldn't be paying me to ask the Service to hold up his refund. And I would have to go see Armand Redfield in Oakland. That required a trip over the bay, and as a transplanted native, I sneered at Oakland the way only a reformed addict can.

Armand and his Service depended on the pure unadulterated honesty of the majority of citizens paying taxes so that the IRS agents could focus on the 3 or 4 percent of tax deadbeats, frauds, and "ideological" objectors who didn't pay or denied the government's moral authority to tax. I then defended and investigated the returns of those so armored by greed, ideology, or secular religion. Righteousness was theirs. And even then half the time the Service was wrong, or at least technically incorrect. My real clients, the guys I got assigned work from, were hotshot tax attorneys. The tax court counterparts to Johnnie Cochran, but without the loud ties and the showman's courtroom demeanor.

They always, and I mean always, had their own tax accounting of their clients done at their own expense. Surprises in the courtroom were death, and their clients' aversion to truth or disclosure was the rule, not the exception. So I got called in as the local green eyeshade. The lawyers could blame me for being a secrecy-obsessed compulsive, a digger of secrets, an explorer of tax guilt. Yes, sir, they told their clients, he should be fired on the spot, will do it tomorrow. But what about this home sale? This was unexpected capital gains? You sold that house in . . . wherever. You thought there was a deduction on capital gains for second homes? But this is a third home, and there have never been any deductions for capital gains on real estate, much less an exclusion, which is what you really meant. So by all means, sir, let's come clean, if not with our family or the IRS, at least between ourselves and Max. I can't defend you without complete honesty. Of course, we acknowledge that Max is obsessive, nasty, insistent, all that. Yes, he's fired. Tomorrow. By tomorrow, I promise.

And with that I would be off to another job, the lawyer paying my bills promptly, the smart ones happy and grateful for taking the ax from their clients. I saved their reputation. They found the saw inside the cake and ate it, too. I got a fast guilty check.

I was in the process of assembling Danny's public records,

his IRS filings and state tax returns, UCC filings, checking them for discrepancies or even new data, any unreported transactions, anything, when my computer whirred to life and an instant message popped up on the screen.

Joe Dempsey calling. I will take a message. Irene.

My eyes found the bay again. The swells were blue green today, not dark, a lightness that came with spring. Sometimes it was hard to believe I lived in the midst of so much beauty. My hands went to the keyboard.

Irene, I'll take it. And no back talk. Okay?

Okay, came the unusually brief reply.

My phone rang. I picked the featherweight handle up slowly.

"Max Smoller," I said, just like . . . Max Smoller, tax detective.

I was almost smiling as I bent my head to the earphone, at least until Irene appeared in the doorway. She leaned her shoulder against the doorjamb and crossed her arms over her chest.

"Joe. How are you?" I said into the phone, as amiably as I could manage, using my eyebrows to play to Irene's spectating.

"Max," came the soft charcoal voice. "Thanks for taking my call. It's been a long time and I . . . well, I didn't know whether you'd take my call."

"I'm still here," I said, reduced to mild truculence.

"How are you?" he asked. "Really. Not your standard phone answer, if you please. You got all my referrals?"

That was Joe all over. The charm offensive, cutting to the chase, something given and something withheld, all at once.

"Yes, Joe, I did." Joe had taken to referring all his hedge fund clients, old and new, retail and wholesale (that's industry jargon for individuals and institutions). It turned out to be the bulk of my practice now, a practice I had grown and tended with careful attention, but which we both knew, and he was reminding me, I probably could not have started without his high-flying imprimatur.

"Got billions under management now. Short-long funds, five or six bond funds, some distressed and bankruptcies." He paused. "But I don't expect you're following my exploits closely. Am I right?"

I could feel my molars start to grind, and pretty soon my dentist would appear in front of me shaking her finger at me like my mother.

"What can I do for you, Joe? Your tax cycle isn't for another six months."

"I was calling—hell, I wasn't calling to see how you are—you know that. I hear Christina called you and you turned her down. Right?"

This time there was silence on my end of the phone, and he let it draw out. Was he calling to convince me where Christina failed? Did he want Christina to fail? Was there something else he wanted? I tried to go through all the permutations of his agenda, combined with the fact that he thought Christina had called in, not written, her plea. With Joe the bottom line was always hidden. His chuckle rumbled in my ear and I heard him break the silence. "I've got a confession, Max. Chris—Christina—and I separated a while back but we got a problem to solve together before we can agree on the papers. The divorce papers."

"I see," was all I could say. I guess I knew where the "Forever Yours" came from now.

"The Service has been on my back about a whole bunch of straddles we did back during the bubble; all those Internet guys trying to move income. You know those, right? And Armand's been lead agent on the audit."

"You seem to be dropping his name a lot."

"Danny finally came to see you?" Joe asked.

"Him and his plastic hand," I said.

"Yeah, he's got this wacky . . . don't worry, Max, he's okay. A little to the right of Attila the Hun. At least what passes for right in California. He actually thinks people should keep what they earn and we should kill people trying to kill us.

"Anyway, Armand's lead, and he goes back three years and checks the returns, which are all legit, but now he's trying to back into 1997 to 2000, even though they're closed and out of legal review, but he's using some gibberish about '01's returns based on fraudulent previous returns and . . . well, you remember Armand."

"Yeah, I remember him." I wanted to stop this monologue before Joe really got a head of steam. "What do you want with me?"

"Christina and I are on the same side on this. We both need your help. Christina doesn't want to see my estate depleted by taxes any more than I do. The bulldog's on our ass, old man. You can't refuse us, can you?"

That was a dirty trick, I thought, the "old man" line. Joe's "old man" referred to the first heady days of our friendship as singles on the Filbert Steps, not too far from where I sat now on the Alcatraz side of Telegraph Hill. We watched *The Third Man* one night and took to calling each other "old man," mimicking Orson Welles's urbane and corrupt smirk and his, "What can I do, old man, I'm dead, aren't I?" Joe was all the way up on Pacific Heights now, in another world of huge mansions—elegant patios, basement swimming pools, rooftop gardens, and indoor squash courts—even in a city where acreage was more expensive than in Manhattan. And I was still here, on Telegraph Hill.

"Joe, I know what you're trying to do."

"Max, they're really on me this time. They're close. They're close to both of us."

"Both of you? How is Christina involved? She'll get a marital pass anyway."

"We're separated, remember?"

"No, Joe. No. I'm sorry. I appreciate everything you've done for me. But there's only so much I owe you. And my dignity's not for sale."

"Max. No one's going to assault your dignity. I'm begging you."

"I wouldn't care if you were King Arthur on bended knee."

"Max, this could take us all down. Just come over tomorrow morning. Take a look at the docs in the data room. You believe I have a locked data room for all these agents? You believe that? That's how many of these fire ants I got crawling up my butt, old man."

"Joe . . ."

"At least have a drink at Marty's. They're your audits anyway. If you still want out after Marty's, well, you can tell Christina yourself. I'll be there by eight."

And he hung up.

Did that mean Christina would be there? Shit. You bastard, old man. You fine, ruthless bastard, bringing Christina into this, bringing back memory. *As if she'd ever been out of it*, I thought. *As if.*

Chapter 4

I arrived at Pier 39's cavalcade of honky-tonks, T-shirt shops, and restaurants as many of them were closing, the gutters filling with a greenish runoff from the kitchens. The water of the bay spread its thick cold smell over the pier. Night had fallen a couple of hours before, and tourists and diners had departed for brighter sights and more vibrant sounds than the lapping of small waves against the darkened piers or the twinkling of Oakland's lights across the bay. I was still amazed at Joe for both his demand to meet tonight and his choice of Pier 39. There was no way he had been here since, well, ten years ago when we were kids at Andersen and not racing toward the brick wall of forty. The places he preferred now were white tablecloths where the maître d' had a long nose out for you if you didn't have on a tie or at least a dark shirt and darker jacket with the black, square patent leather shoes of downtown fashion.

Marty's Wharf Bar didn't come up to Joe's interior design standards, either. There were typical nautical accoutrements—nets, spindled wheels, brass compasses—and the distinctly unnautical smell of disinfectant and cleaning fluid. Standing behind the bar was a girl in a long ponytail who scarcely looked old enough to drink and would certainly have been carded if she had walked into the empty cavernous room above. As I headed for the bar, the netting hanging from the ceiling made me want to duck even though it cleared my head by a good ten feet.

Joe was already there, hunched over something dark, with flecks of silver from ice cubes reflected through glass. I could see his long shoulders and knees at odd angles as if he could not get comfortable on the seat when he twisted to see me. He sat up straight, aware of being appraised. His toothy smile shone white in the gleaming dark of the bar while a neon Budweiser sign cast a faint red glow behind him. My pace quickened. My hand came up of its own accord. Even now, as he straightened off the stool and his smile cleared and his chin tilted, waiting for my anger or recrimination or coldness, even now as I saw his wariness of me, my hand came up and my heart lightened despite itself and the scalding memory of when he left with Christina. Through all that, I still was glad to see him. His hand came out, too. I felt his strong grip and the muscles going up his arm. He pulled me into the bar and into a brief embrace in the crook of his left arm.

"Max," he said. "Good to see you. I wasn't sure you would come."

"Me neither. What's with meeting in this dive?"

He looked around and a grin creased his mouth and twisted up the crow's-feet at his eyes. There was gray at his temples. I could see it even in the dim bar. That was new, at least five years new anyhow. Someone put on music, and Costello's throaty, lonely voice filled the clink of glasses being placed on the rack by the girl behind the bar.

"I never come to places like this," he said. "Thought it would bring back old times."

"Joe, don't start with bullshit. You wouldn't come here if your life depended on it, and you wouldn't lean on me or work so hard to get me here to this dive if something wasn't wrong. What the hell do you want?"

"Nice to know you haven't changed, Max. Still not putting up with the social conventions."

"Social *lies* you mean."

He stood firing-squad straight. He had waited for my volley, and now that it had come, he seemed surprised. I was. Just a second ago I had felt that familiar undertow of affection and excitement. He nodded.

"I guess I deserve that," he said.

"Look, Joe, I'm not here to . . . to go over old ground. Just tell me what you want and why you called."

He sighed. "All right, if that's the way it feels best for you." He raised the first two fingers of his right hand and waved lazily at the bartender, then turned back to me.

"Things are bad."

"You said that on the phone. Call some lawyers. You have plenty. Call her accountants. You can buy any one of those. Call all those people who jump when you raise a pinky finger."

"It's not like that. It's worse."

"Worse than not paying your taxes?" I said.

"Look, Max, it's not about taxes; I mean, yes, it's the IRS thugs, but they think someone's . . . they're trying to pin me with bribing officials."

"You bribed an official?"

"No. No way. Do you think I'm that fuckin' stupid?"

"I never thought so. Why are they leaning on you then?"

The bartender put a fresh glass of Lagavulin on the bar. The old-fashioned tumbler had his preferred two ice cubes in it, and the girl shot Joe an appraising glance, but he didn't catch it. Joe had rarely missed a look like that before. He lifted his glass and swirled the amber liquor, then said, "Because I've got a lot of investors. Rich guys. Very high net worth. They've been . . . I've been doing tax straddles for these guys. They're aggressive about it."

"So? That still doesn't explain why the IRS is coming after you."

"They think I knew what these guys were doing!"

"Did you?"

"No. How many times do I have to tell you? No way. I just did the straddles. It's all legal. They're not my fucking returns."

"The same old crap: Not my job. Not my responsibility. Not my tax returns."

"Don't you get high and mighty on me. You're a tax accountant. Not a tax *lawyer*."

"Well. It finally comes out. The famous Joe Dempsey arrogance. People always told me about it. But I guess the charm never slipped in front of me before, right?"

Joe grabbed his drink off the glossy wood of the bar and tossed the ice and booze into his mouth. He brought his jaw down on the ice, and the crunching sound popped between us. The muscles in his jaw bunched, and from the side I could see real fire in his eyes. He pushed out a lungful of air and dropped the glass on the bar. The bartender trotted from the other end and poured another double shot of single malt into the empty glass. She held up a spoonful of ice. Joe nodded. As the ice fell, I watched. Joe was scared. And I'd never seen him scared. Scared enough to lose the charm, to drop the wit, to freeze the easy smile.

I saw him pull himself back, braced by another slug from the tumbler. His tongue flicked out to lick his lips. He kept looking at the glass, turning it with his hand.

Talking just loud enough for me to hear, as the bartender returned to her station, he said, "The Service thinks I've been making payoffs to get favorable treatment and keep these straddles from being audited."

"Have you?" I asked again.

"No." He turned to me. "Jesus."

I saw fear in his eyes again and I couldn't help but feel the hardness loosening in my chest.

"I don't know what I can do."

"You're the only one I trust. Because you're not . . . my friend."

"You mean because I'm not an employee, or a customer," I said. "What are they after?"

"They say they're after me. But I think they want me to roll over and tell them about my investors. Typical thuglike behavior from the Service, you know."

"The Service stopped doing that years ago."

"I know, but they put Redfield on it."

"It's bad to get a bounce like that out of the starting gate, but he can't find something that's not there."

"I'm clean, Max. I swear. I mean, in the bribery stuff. I'm not saying the straddle wasn't aggressive."

"Maybe it's just personal then."

"No. He keeps asking about Kessler and Stoppard."

"You got them?"

"Yeah. They're the ones I've been doing straddles for. You

have to talk to him. At least Armand knows you won't lie. Even for me."

"Okay, Joe. I'll come over to the office in the morning and take a look at the docs. But Armand's right about one thing."

"What's that?"

"I won't lie. Even for you."

"You mean especially for me."

"Maybe I do," I said. I slid away from the bar and left him looking into his glass.

"I should have invited you to the wedding, old man," he said, still looking down.

I said, "I'll see you tomorrow." And I turned away. I could see him throw a look at me in the mirror and jut his chin in some kind of troubled acknowledgment.

I walked out and found mist. The fog had descended and covered the green oily water in the gutters, and the neon signs glowed red behind the wet haze. My footsteps muffled themselves until I reached my car and sparked the engine into life.

Chapter 5

Joe Dempsey's office was over past Union Square across the street from the old *Chronicle* building, a squat fortress of granite on the ragged edge of the Mission District. Built in the '30s under a WPA grant, the building's huge stones were stacked together with exquisite care. Now it straddled the skyscrapers of the financial district and the disaster of San Francisco's Mission, its abandoned lots, the homeless trailing pushcarts, dealers and customers using the streets as store, bedroom, and toilet.

Even though Joe's office was on the edge of the Mission, it didn't straddle. It was squarely downtown: black leather, blond wood, secretaries in tight skirts and loose shirts, or loose skirts and tight shirts, phones ringing off the hook, and a huge cavernous bullpen where traders bought, sold, and originated the mortgages and debt securities that were the lifeblood of his business. He had built it up from a storefront to a corner office in the financial district over the ten years after Andersen, until he bought the building and converted it to his own image. He said he wanted to give something back. I always figured it for just one more of Joe's angles. A tax rebate, a tax-free office for the mayor down on the twentieth floor, something.

The elevators opened and bedlam wafted over me. But it wasn't the bullpen chaos with traders shouting over computer banks with phones welded to their ears. The traders all sat at their desks, some with heads in their hands. Assistants had puffy eyes. Uniformed cops stood at the elevator and ran to and fro across the bullpen. A big cop with pale skin and Asian features stood next to the marble reception desk, his hands on his belt. The receptionist spoke slowly into her headset, her wide eyes on the cop, having an out-of-body experience as she put calls through to the maelstrom in the bullpen and the walls crumbled around her. A bunch of guys in white shirts and dark ties and gray pants were lugging boxes past me. One man, a balding jar cut with beefeater arms, barreled past me, clipping me with a corner of a cardboard box full of files.

"Where are you going with those?"

"Who are you?" he asked.

"Are those Joe's files?"

"Who. Are. You," he said, spacing it out. He turned around and pushed the box closer to me. He held it at chest level, forcing me to take a step back.

"Where's Joe?" I asked

He turned with the box and faced the reception area.

"Tony?"

One of the blue uniforms stuck his head around a door frame. "Yeah?"

He tilted his head at me.

"ID this guy, will you?"

"Sure."

He turned back to me, then put the box down on the corner of a desk. He waited for Tony.

Tony walked up to me with small, careful steps and stopped a couple of yards away and spread his feet. He hooked a thumb in his belt on his gun side. There was a creak of leather in the silence.

"My name is Max Smoller," I said.

I reached into my coat pocket for my wallet. I tugged out my driver's license. Tony took a step toward me and grabbed it, his thumb, nail bitten down to the quick, on top. He turned it toward him with an awkward arm twist, keeping his hand on his belt.

"What's your business here, Mr. Smoller?"

"I'm Joe Dempsey's accountant."

"You have an appointment?"

"No. I doubt I was on his schedule. I just wanted to talk to him. We're old friends."

Tony looked over at the man, who was picking up the box again.

"Mr. Guthrie?"

Guthrie nodded. Tony stepped back to me, handed me back my license, with his arm at his side. The tension drained out of his stance.

"How long have you known Mr. Dempsey?" asked Guthrie.

"I've been doing his taxes since he started," I said. I looked into the box he was holding. It had manila folders with the tabs facing me. They were all numbered by year.

"Joe didn't do anything wrong," I said, nodding at the box. "I'm sure his taxes were in order. I did them myself."

"I think we'll find out," Guthrie said. "You do Joe's clients also?"

I shrugged and said, "Some."

"How many?"

"Enough. What's this about?"

Guthrie turned his ice-blue eyes at me, and I watched a quietness behind them that I couldn't place.

"Come with me," he said.

I followed without asking the questions filling my thoughts. They couldn't get past my lips. Guthrie lugged the box out to reception and handed it to Tony, who was standing around, watching everyone and writing in a little spiral notebook. Tony took it. I finally got a question out. "Where are we going?"

"2305 Divisadero."

"Joe's house?"

"That's right."

"Who are you?"

Guthrie turned to me, the questions still in the air, a look of surprise on his face. He put out a square hand, big and soft. "I'm Terry Guthrie, district attorney."

"Why are we going to Joe's?"

"Because Joe's over there."

"Joe didn't do anything. He may be aggressive but he never crosses the line," I said. "I never let him."

"We'll check his records. If what you say is true, I'm sure there'll be no problem." He kept moving. "Your car downstairs?"

We were out of the lobby, standing in front of the elevator bank. Guthrie shrugged into his suit coat, then raised a brown felt Stetson from his side and settled it on his head with his fingers holding the crown.

"Your car outside?" he asked again.

I nodded. It seemed like that was all I could do.

"I got the gray Chevy out front. You can follow me."

The ride down was silent except for the hum of the elevator dropping us forty floors in twenty seconds, almost as fast as a free fall. It stopped before we broke our legs.

Out on the street he pointed out a late model Caprice, the tires without whitewalls betraying it as government issue. The white business plate with "California Government" stamped in the right corner didn't help, either. I followed him out of the Mission, up Van Ness and into Pacific Heights until we hit the crest of Divisadero, then on to Joe's.

We got out in bright sunshine that had gone unnoticed in the shade of the tall buildings downtown. Joe's stone and stucco mansion dazzled in the sun, its windows blinking. There were three squad cars parked out front and an unmarked white van in the driveway. I squinted into a building headache and followed Guthrie's broad back up Joe's white terrazzo steps to the open door.

When I stepped through the antique oak double doors and into the black-and-white marble foyer, there were a couple of cops in uniforms standing around. More men in white shirts and ties wore rubber gloves. My feet stopped of their own accord. My heart started hammering. Insistent. Guthrie turned and faced me, with his back to the staircase sweeping upward.

"We tried to find someone else," he said. "But we couldn't."

"Someone else?"

"It's bad news. I'm afraid your friend Joe is dead," he said. I heard the words, and I heard other things, my heart thudding, of course, a leaking faucet in the bathroom down the hall, or a toilet running. But the stupid thing was the quiet. And the pressure. I felt like I had come down from forty thousand feet and hadn't been able to clear my ears. Like I wanted someone to bang me on the head if it wouldn't stop.

Guthrie took my elbow and led me up the stairs. I watched the floor railing come level with my head as if I were on some hidden machinery. I had no sensation of my legs moving. He turned to me, the quietness in his eyes, all over his face, all over me. I took a step back and the banister, waist level now, stopped me from falling down the stairwell.

"He's in great shape," I said.

Guthrie nodded. "He's dead."

"He runs twenty miles a week. Marathons. Bikes up mountains. Softball games. Squash. Something every day. Every day. He's a fanatic. His blood pressure is a hundred five over seventy-five, standing heart rate forty-five."

"He played softball?" Guthrie asked.

"He plays in a league, with the guys from Firehouse 241." Christina used to sit on the sidelines in jeans and a sweatshirt; she managed to look as put together as if she wore a Chanel suit.

"I know. I'm sorry, but he's dead, Max. We need you to help us."

I nodded.

"Heart attack? Like Fixx?" Jim Fixx was the fitness runner guru who dropped dead of a heart attack while jogging, back in the 1980s.

"No. I'm sorry. He was murdered," said Guthrie. "With his softball bat," he added.

I shook my head. "There's no way," I said. "No way."

I reached for the railing then, held on to it for all it was worth. I put my head down on its cool grained walnut, as if its immovability could create something to ground me. My legs got rubbery and I sat down on the carpet abruptly with my back against the wall and put my head between my knees.

"It's a positive ID. Prints. We'll get the DNA back in a couple of days. Everything," Guthrie said. "I know it's hard to believe."

"He was only forty-three," I said. "Is he still here?"

"No. We took him downtown."

I sat with my head between my knees and looked at the carpet. When my breathing settled, I leaned back and bounced the back of my head on the wall. The pain felt sweet somehow, though I didn't do it for long.

"Why am I here?" I asked Guthrie, who towered over me.

"We need your help with his files." I stared up at him.

"I told you. His taxes are in order. I did most of them myself except for the last couple of years."

"Come over and look at this."

He put out a hand, but I rolled onto a knee and pushed myself up with a hand on the wall. He turned quickly and walked down the hall to the double doors that led to the master bedroom.

Joe had laughed when the designer showed the double bedroom doors on the plans.

"What chick's gonna want to walk through some colonnade to get to my bedroom?" he said. "I'll never get laid here. You got to slide them in, not announce it like some coronation." But he let them talk him into it. He and Christina were still a dry brushfire waiting for lightning to strike, or a match. I never thought she would walk through that doorway, or that Joe would invite her.

The doors were open and the French windows had gauzy draped linen over them. I could see Joe's view of the bay and the Sausalito hills. The bed was stripped, and the cover was spread out on the floor on the left side. To the right was a huge, amoebic stain on the rug, its edge climbing the mattress. I could see where it had crusted in the fiber pile. My chest started thudding again. I broke out in a cold sweat that started in my stomach, the kind you get when your blood sugar's low and you feel hollow and shaky. In the corner was a cherry table desk with some books, an Apple laptop, assorted writing tools. On one corner lay a lefty first baseman's glove. Underneath the desk in the corner of the wall was a scuffed softball. There was no chair at the desk, and it made me angry. His lone desk, denuded, stripped like the room. Like Joe's future. Like mine.

"Where's the chair?" I asked Guthrie. He shrugged, then turned and waited and put his hands behind his back. "Where's the goddamn chair?"

"They probably took it," he said softly.

A tech walked through the room, dressed in jeans and a button-down shirt with the sleeves rolled up. His arms were covered with dense black hair, and it was matted against the clear plastic gloves he wore up to the elbows. He looked at Guthrie with a frown and downward tilt to his head, like a schoolteacher disappointed in a star pupil. Guthrie looked back at him.

"We'll be done in a minute."

"There's no need," he said, picked up a pen lying on the desk, and left. I couldn't figure out whether he meant there was no need to leave or to be here at all. Guthrie walked over to the desk and unlocked a drawer. He pulled it out, then lifted files that had powder and smudges all over them.

Guthrie searched for a clean place to put them, then finally put them on top of the desk and flipped them open.

"This is Joe's?" he asked. I took a step toward the desk. I didn't want to get any closer. I didn't want to get under the surface of things. I wanted somebody else to clean up Joe's stuff and I wanted to go home and soak in Scotch or eat Valium or inhale my stack of weed or stare at baseball games on the television for a week. Anything to bludgeon reality back into submission. "Is it your work?" asked Guthrie.

I sidled closer.

I was close enough to the desk to see the file. Inside was a photocopy of a will. The opening paragraphs had the usual preambles, the obligatory whereases. It was not hard to read the heading: Last Will and Testament of Mr. Joseph Edwards Dempsey.

"No," I said.

"You're sure? I thought you did his tax work," Guthrie said, a crease forming at his mouth where he seemed to taste something sour.

"I did. But no estate work. I could have done some tax planning. Once his will was settled."

"So who did this?"

"Joe did it. Probably."

"He's not a lawyer."

"He passed the bar."

"But he didn't practice?"

"No. Never even applied to law school. He passed the bar exam on his first try, but he never bothered to get admitted."

"Why in the world did he start as an accountant?"

I smiled. I had asked him the very same thing. We had been down in that shithole of offices that Arthur Andersen had on Market, where the cubicles were tilting at asymmetric angles and the walls wobbled whenever Joe or I tacked a piece of paper on them. He had silently passed over the wall between us the congratulatory letter from the State Bar.

"So. You gonna be a big tax lawyer now?" I asked.

"Nah, you got to be able to do the numbers yourself," he said.

"That's what people hire us for."

"You ever talk to rich people?" he asked.

"Sure, Joe. I walk up to them all the time. They love talking about how they made their money. How rich they are."

"You noticed that, too?"

I snorted. "I wasn't serious."

"Oh." His face split in a grin that had no sheepishness in it at all. "They do, you know. If you ask them, they'll talk about it for hours. Tell you all their secrets."

"That right?" I asked.

"Every one."

"So what's the secret?" I said.

"To what?" he asked.

"Getting rich, dummy."

He lost his tiny smile, the one that held his face most of the time, that most people took for a smirk. He loved thinking, wondering where he was going to end up. He was pretty sure it was going to be somewhere good.

"I don't think there is a secret. Some of these rich guys are dumb as posts. Some are lights-out smart. Some are lucky. Some are workaholics. I don't think there's a special sauce."

"So if there's no secret, how are you so sure it'll happen to you?"

He spread his hands wide. He pointed his thumbs at himself, as his suit jacket parted revealing his shiny belt and suspenders, a street carnie hawking his wares to customers wishing for magic.

"If not me, then who?" he had said.

Everything seemed to break his way. His contacts at the corporations, the CFOs, loved him. The partners at Andersen wouldn't dump him because they couldn't believe they were holding on to a guy who should've been a managing director at Goldman Sachs or the youngest mergers and acquisitions partner at Wachtell, Lipton. The accounting partners were watching their business leaching away, their margins plummeting, their liabilities skyrocketing, their lawsuits multiplying, as their best people deserted accounting. Accountants have a major inferiority complex, with good reason.

Joe just thought his own path led through accounting, not law or banking like every other schmuck from Harvard Business School did. He was going to make it big, and he knew the ticket was his own company.

"So Joe did this will?" asked Guthrie, back in the room, quiet with the techs gone now and the dark splotch hovering in the middle of the room, a repulsive magnet. I turned back to the desk.

"It seems like Joe's drafting. It's really simple anyway. If you know what you want to do with it. The hard part is getting trustees you trust."

"And you're a trustee?"

"I was, but Joe and I haven't been close for a few years. If it's new, he probably did the trusts, but it's really simple, like I told you."

"Joe didn't know estate law or taxes?"

"It wasn't his specialty. He was more focused on financial accounting and reporting, SEC stuff."

"And his mother was the beneficiary?"

"On the first one I did for him, but now it's probably Christina. Just look for yourself," I said.

"We did."

I grabbed the will out of Guthrie's hand. "The signature of the notary and witnesses are right here," I said, turning to the last page. I saw the spiky hand, Christina Ethel Lawson.

"You see this new one and these papers?" Guthrie asked, the muscles on the side of his jaw working and popping, giving his head an even squarer look, if that was possible.

"Letters of Administration," I said. "Papers you file with the court if someone dies."

"I know what those are. Maybe I didn't pass the bar without law school, but I am the DA. In this state that still means a law degree. I want to know why they're here. And why this new will doesn't mention Christina."

"Okay," I said.

I took another breath and said, "I don't have a clue. Joe liked—he felt better with all the cards facing him. He didn't like secrets exactly. He just didn't like giving out personal information. He wouldn't have told me all this stuff."

Guthrie nodded and, taking the will, riffled back a few pages. "Take a look at this then." He flipped to the second paragraph and stopped at a familiar name, mine. I was listed as sole trustee.

He handed back the document. I held it for a second. I flipped again to the last page. Ms. Christina Ethel Lawson, currently residing at 2305 Divisadero, had signed. There was a scrawled notary's signature and a date, March 15, 2001. Two years ago. The new one was undated. Joe hadn't said exactly when they separated; another hidden cost.

Guthrie said, "You know her? Christina Lawson?"

I nodded, still holding the will in my hand. "A bit."

There was a slight breeze in the room. One of the techs had opened the double doors to air out the smell of chemicals and the copper smell of blood and the heat from the camera lights. The breeze rustled at the papers in my hand.

"She was living here," he said.

I looked at Guthrie. "With Joe?" I stared. "They weren't separated?"

"Wet toothbrush. Fancy pumps. Full makeup drawers. It would be hard to call that 'separated.' Did you think they were?"

I nodded, but I did not know how to speak. I was watching Christina's letter flutter airily down to my desk, her throaty imagined voice in my ear. And Joe's flowing charm. There was an icy flush creeping up from my navel. I nodded again.

"He implied they were separated," I said.

Guthrie pursed his lips, the calmness coming over his face again. This time there was a light, a sharpness in them I didn't like too much. I handed him back the document. He looked down at it, breaking his gaze.

"You're going to have to go down to the city lockup if you want to talk to her."

"What?"

"Jail," he said. "Fifth Street and Bryant, off Market."

"Why?"

"Her prints were all over the place."

"She lived here!"

"I thought you only knew her 'a bit'?"

"You said she lived here," I said, my voice came out low and controlled, like a big cat before it growls.

"Her prints were all over the bat. She was covered with blood."

"She probably just found the body, for God's sake."

"Good guess. We had to book her."

"You had to throw her in jail?" I shook my head and looked down at the carpet. "Jesus Christ." I turned and marched down the steps, then turned around at the first landing. "What the hell'd you do that for?" My heels thudded on every step going down and I could feel the fear build with each progression. Guthrie called back from the top of the stairs.

"You can get her bail, if she hasn't got it already, and she'll be out by dinnertime," he said. "But you better find her a good lawyer."

I started for the door.

"And maybe one for yourself," he said, watching my eyes from above as I looked up. I held his gaze and wiped all fear from my face, because it was a bluff.

I knew she could use a lawyer. If he asked for my alibi, I would call a lawyer. He knew it too. A cop would root around for how long and how well I knew Christina, that was normal. Though I knew where to find lawyers, all kinds, his words hung in the air like smoke from a guilty cigarette. I turned away from him and went through Joe's front door and down his steps to the street. The black-and-whites were all gone. My Audi wagon nosed close to the rear of Guthrie's beaten-up Chevy, until I got in and reversed it away.

I remember thinking to myself, *I have to work this out. No way could Christina do this. She was . . . she was not someone who could. Do what?* I asked myself. *What?* But driving in the car up and down the hills didn't clear my mind. My thoughts chorused up and down while the Audi dropped and rolled down California Street and Nob Hill back to my office on Sutter, where there was a phone I could work and an attorney I could call.

Chapter 6

I went down to the Fifth Street station, a redbrick building on the city's dulled edge, torn between Moscone Center and the gentrified district around the ballpark. The cop at the desk pointed me mutely to a glass-walled room with benches around the side and a desk with a painfully gaunt woman in a cop uniform, gray streaks in her black hair. Behind was a steel door with a glass pane. She looked up at me with eyes so black I couldn't distinguish between iris and pupil and gave me no room or quarter. She waited. I shoved her the slip of paper the cop at the front had given me, which I pushed through a grate in the glass wall.

Through the wire-stitched glass I could see barred holding rooms. Against one back wall I could see Christina curled on a bench, her legs drawn up under her and her blond hair matted and twisted into haphazard braids that made it dark.

Her face pointed away from me to the wall, and I watched an errant hand come up and twirl the ends of her hair into more tangles. She kept twirling her hair around an index finger, staring at the wall.

The cop at the table rapped her knuckles on the metal and read out loud from the paper into a microphone. "Lawson," she said.

Christina's hand stopped, and for a moment she was still. Then her neck muscles roped under the skin, and her head picked up and twisted. She saw us then but put her head back down on her hand. She looked at the woman, then at me, then at the woman again.

"You're out," the woman said, pressing a button on the wall. A buzzer sounded and Christina's door clunked open.

Christina rolled herself up and pushed at her legs. She walked up to the door and then came through it.

"Max," she said, working her tongue over her lips. "You're here."

"Let's get you out of here, Christina," I said, my voice croaking as if I hadn't used it in months.

"I can go?" she asked the cop.

"What I said," she replied, then softened. "You can pick up your stuff at the window. Right turn at the end of the hall."

Christina shuffled over to me, her jail slippers sliding across the concrete. I looked down at her.

"My shoes," she said, grimacing. Even here, her beauty hit me again, hit me with a thunk square in the chest, right on the breastbone, an inch or so under my sternum. It spread like a red tide outward until I could feel it flush my skin, setting up a pleasant tingle and then a hollow in the pit of my stomach. I swallowed a couple of times to make it go away. But her green eyes were surrounded by gold with flecks of emerald in them, and they looked at me, and my faint blushing spread. I grabbed her arm for something to hold on to.

"C'mon, let's get you out of here."

"I just need my shoes," she said. "And my belt. They took my belt." She blinked several times. One side of her face was dimpled, from resting on her knee, I thought. There was a bulge to her left eye that betrayed exhaustion.

"Like the airlines," I said. "They treat you okay?"

"They took my watch too. Even the airlines don't do that."

The cop looked up and said, "Only a few hours. Coulda been worse."

I nodded while Christina shuffled out the door and we turned down the hall. At the cage I showed the slip of paper again, and they brought her shoes and belt and purse and watch in a plastic tray, the kind you put your wallet in at airport security. She signed the piece of paper they pushed at her and bent over to put on her cork-soled sandals, then shoved the paper slippers into a garbage can waiting at the side of the cage.

Another woman behind the cage took the paper and pulled out a pair of reading glasses that she perched on a petite but red-rimmed nose. Her eyes looked over the paper.

"Your court date is set. Twenty-first of next month. Until then you're on your own recognizance. You understand that?" Christina nodded.

"That means you don't show and they'll get you and then won't set bail." She looked back at the paper. "Bond's already a hundred grand; that your sugar here putting it up?" she said, grinning at me, the slack skin on her face jiggling.

I elbowed Christina aside and stuck my face into the cage. "At least she's got one," I said.

Then I took Christina's arm and led her down the hall and out into the sunshine. Away from the narrow halls, from the glass cage, from the smell of sweat, disinfectant, and urine, and from the baked-in smell of fear. Outside, a hedge of star jasmine refreshed the street, and the white flowers dripped on the sidewalk.

There was noise in the street, too, more than cars and horns. Vague shouts from megaphones and bullhorns wafted through the alleys between buildings, and when we drove across Market we could see demonstrators congregating for an antiwar march. White banners of "Down with War," "Down with Bush," "No WMDs," and a raft of other slogans were strung across the street. A couple of hundred people milled about, listening intermittently to a woman standing on a garbage can shouting instructions through a megaphone.

We drove in my car through the press of people, and through my open window I heard an organizer coaching people on how to get released, insist on a lawyer, have someone ready with bail money.

I headed the car through them as they parted for us, touching the car's windows and flanks. Then we were free, in the relative emptiness of Market Street traffic on a quiet Saturday morning. I turned up Divisadero toward Joe's house.

"Where should we go?" I asked.

Christina sat silently, a black-holed aura sucking light and energy through the windshield, oblivious to everything around her. I tried again. "Christina, where do you want to go?"

"I don't know," she said, shrugging. "Take me anywhere." I pulled the car out into traffic.

"Do you need clothes?"

There was no answer. Christina looked at a street sign and turned to me for the first time. I tried to meet her eyes. They were dull and wandering, her right eye unconnected with her left. *She never had a lazy eye, did she?* I thought. "Not Joe's," she said.

45

Maybe I should have paid more attention to that wandering eye. But I knew she needed rest and thought she was just exhausted.

"Right," I said. What an idiot. I was going to take her back to Joe's for clothes? There were barely any left after being impounded as evidence, the rest filthy with fingerprint powder or just the ugly paws of techs and assorted men rifling through Joe's house, Joe's old life. Christina's too.

I turned the car back, away from Pacific Heights, and fled downhill and downtown to our unknown destination.

"Where should we go?" No answer again. "Where would you like to sleep? Do you need stuff?"

She kept looking ahead.

She asked, "Do you still have that parakeet? Captain Black? The ugly one?"

"Captain Flag. And his nose was broken was all."

She nodded. No smile that I could see. Rare for her. "No, he died a year ago or so. Do you need clothes, Christina?"

She shrugged, an adolescent who withholds an obvious and direct answer from an obtuse parent.

"Should I take you to a friend's house? What about Leslie? That girl who you were pals—friends with?"

"I haven't seen her in a while. We're still friends. Her family's big here in town. They'll know." She paused. "They knew Joe."

"I see."

"If you don't know anyplace," she said, and stopped, turning to look at me. She waited. The silence built. I held my breath. "Then I'll try a hotel tonight," she said. We tilted at an ominous angle, going down the spine of the Heights, and I had the crazy sense we would fall off the planet, all bearings lost.

I let a deep breath out through my nose and lips quietly as I turned onto California. The street flattened out, we passed the Pacific Union Club on top of Nob Hill, the hood of the car crested the hill, and all I could see was sky. Then it nosed over and we were rolling downward, and I rode the brakes the whole way.

At the bottom I said, "Let's get you some overnight clothes first."

Christina nodded again and sat back against the leather seat. I almost opened my mouth to say something, but I kept it clamped tight. It was better this way, much better. So I turned the car back again and went up Sutter, navigating the hills, heading for Union Square.

We stopped at Union Square, and the pitching and falling of the car's nose eased, a ship finally making port, and I drove her to the Ritz-Carlton, her favorite and the most expensive aerie in the city, with a full minibar of liquor and obsequious service, perfect for a person of her standing in the community. She would quickly dial the concierge for overnight clothes from Neiman's, and CVS for toiletries.

But what was she now? Half a power couple? A divorcée? A suspect? I watched her small figure retreat into the cavernous lobby, my questions about her hanging in the air. Questions I wasn't sure I wanted answers to.

My mind chose the route back to the office while I fingered Guthrie's card in my pocket and his admonition echoed in my head: "Get your friend a good lawyer." I called Arthur Lewman's office and made an appointment for 9 a.m.

Chapter 7

Guthrie's voice was still ringing in my ears, so around eight I drove down Broadway to Columbus, passed the Purple Onion, and found half a parking space that I jammed into near Lewman's office building. It was a two-story brick affair in a gentrified section a couple of blocks from the frayed sleaze of the Condor Club on lower Broadway. On the empty sidewalk outside the slick lobby, I pressed buttons on the steel intercom set into the thick, creep-proof glass.

A crisp voice said "Yes?" into the phone and waited. I leaned forward and said, "Arthur Lewman, please. It's Max Smoller." There was another pause.

"Your appointment's at nine," the voice said. "I don't suppose you can wait till then." It was not a question.

"Who are you?"

"Arthur Lewman." Then a buzzer sounded and the lock in the door clicked. I stabbed my hand at the door just quick enough to get it open. After searching the lobby's directory, I stepped onto the elevator and got off on the second floor. Arthur Lewman, Esquire, greeted me at the entrance, all gleaming shoes and red suspenders, with an expression on his face like I had left dirty dishes in the kitchen sink.

I stopped in front of him. "I'm in a hurry," I said.

"Four messages last night? That much was obvious."

"Christina needs a trial lawyer. And she's not your client yet."

There was a brief silence as he considered my opening move, but one that still made me nervous.

"I'd be happy to refer several very experienced lawyers."

"I called you."

"So your messages indicated."

"Look, Mr. Lewman. I know you used to get all the high-profile cases out here. Then you did the Washington thing."

"Deputy attorney general."

"Right. I mean no disrespect, sir, but here's my concern. You've got a big practice. Lots of high-profile cases."

"Your facts are correct."

"This is just a case for you. It's Christina's life. Do you have time to represent her?"

"You mean: Will I do it personally? As well or better than anyone else?"

"It's a murder charge."

"A capital crime," he said. I didn't need reminding. He turned and led the way down the corridor to what looked like a second lobby, except it was paneled in wood, had travertine flooring with Asian rugs, and four desks facing each other. He walked right through them to another door, already open, and disappeared from view. His voice floated out at me. "Come in," he said.

I walked in and took a dimpled leather chair. He was already parked behind a huge partners desk with inlaid leather, his briefcase in the unused kneehole.

"The papers this morning said she was taken into custody right away," he continued. "Is that correct?"

"As far as I know."

"Then she needs help. There must be good evidentiary reasons why they booked her so fast."

"I know she needs help. That's why I called four times."

"We need to stay calm, Mr. Smoller."

"My name is Max. And I am calm."

"I see," he said, as I heard my own breathing whistle through my nose.

"Look, I'm sorry. This is a lot of stress."

"Why?"

"Why what?"

"Why is it a lot of stress?"

"Don't you think a murder is stressful?" I asked.

"Not for me. Why is it for you? Do you know Christina?"

"Of course. Why do you think I called you?"

"How well?"

I heard my own breathing again. "I used to know her. We dated at one time. Does that matter?" I wasn't going into the whole roiled history with him.

"And when did you first become acquainted with her?"

"Mr. Lewman, we're not in a courtroom."

"Forgive me," he said. "I have a bad habit of lapsing into interrogation-speak."

"Arthur," I said, but stopped. There really wasn't anywhere to go with this. If I kept asking, he'd just back off or, worse, say no.

"Mr. Smoller, I . . ."

"Max."

"Max. I will take the case. But first, I must know something."

"What?" I said into his second abrupt silence, as if he had stopped an unpleasant truth from flying out of his mouth. It was hard to finish sentences for a man you hardly knew.

"What's your connection to Christina?"

"Christina's my connection to Christina. And Joe. Joe's a connection to Christina."

"You seem a little *involved* to me."

"Involved? What does that mean?"

"Emotionally involved."

"I am *not* emotionally involved with Christina. I haven't seen her for five years. Yes, we dated. But I was Joe's friend longer than I knew Christina. Much longer."

"I see." More silence. This time I let it sit. It was a hard sit.

After we listened to each other's breathing for a while, he finally continued. "Okay, I'll defend her. But what about you?"

"What about me?"

"What are you going to do?"

"I'm doing it. I got Christina out, signed a guarantee for her bail. I got you. What else is there to do?"

"Many things. Prepare her defense. Corroborate the police investigation. Interviews. Searches"—he stopped, then added—"of financial records."

"You must have worked with dozens of people who do all that."

"Yes and no. I can get someone to cover the police side if we need it. But the financial records, knowledge of Joe's business? It seems to me you're in the best position to do that."

"Me? No way."

"Who else? That's the best thing in these cases. When you're in front of a jury, someone must pay. A murder trial is an exercise in collective revenge. If you don't understand that, you make the jury choose between unsatisfied justice and personal innocence. A terrible choice."

"Innocence is a bad choice?"

"Are you going to stay with the case?" He asked.

"Do I have a choice?"

"Of a kind," he said.

"Not a very comfortable kind."

"No," he said.

I looked around the office for a glass; my throat had suddenly become as dry as a tax return. "Do you have any water?" I asked. He looked at me as if I were eight and had confused subtraction with addition in math class. He turned around without taking his eyes off me, opened a small refrigerator, and grasped a plastic bottle. When he came out with it, he saw the liquid was light brown. "Green tea, I'm afraid. An enthusiasm of mine," he said. I grabbed it and drank.

When the bottle was half empty, I took a deep breath through my nose. The air jetted out of my mouth as if a balloon had ruptured.

"All right, what is it you need me to do?"

"First, find out about the intricacies of Joe's business. Not just what he told you. Then find his partners, his clients, his competitors, his will; most of all—find the dirt. Whether it's women or a Swiss bank account."

"The DA showed me his will, witnessed by Christina. There were Letters of Administration in the file."

"Letters of Administration? Why would they be in Joe's file? If he had a will already?"

"Not sure. Maybe he was going to sign another. He told me they were separated."

"The DA won't care. They'll use the current one. Establish motive. They've got her at the scene?"

"Pretty much," I said. "I haven't really talked to her yet."

"Now you understand why you must help? If you are sincere in your statements of motive."

"Christina didn't do it. And Joe was my friend. An old friend. A lot of blood spilled between us. But an old friend. He didn't deserve to die like that."

"Nobody does," said Arthur.

"Yes," I said. But it happens all the time. One minute people are thinking about what's for dinner, and the next day they're trying to put the world back in place. Happens all the time.

Chapter 8

When I got to the office the next morning, the paperwork for Lewman's engagement was on Irene's desk. I wanted to ask her about it when her expression stopped me.

"You look like shit, Max."

"Good morning to you, too," I said. But it didn't deflect her. The black eyes kept looking at me. "I didn't sleep well last night," I added. I felt my shoulders hunch as I walked wearily into my office, trying to shut the door behind me with a flick of my hand. When there was no noise, I turned around. A couple of long steps got Irene over to my desk. She grabbed my arm.

"Look in the mirror, will you?"

She dragged me over to my exposed, postmodern sink, which had a mirror, a toothbrush hanging next to it, and a shaver out-let, for mornings like this. I admit it was not a pretty sight. My hair was standing straight. The cowlick in back would make Alfalfa run from the room in red-faced shame. I looked at my face for a long moment, studying it for once, a course I always cut when I could.

I smoothed the cowlick in back with the same furtive pat I used to get before school from my mother, who managed to appear hopeful and worried at the same time. If it was truly ungovernable, she'd smooth it down with a tongue-wetted palm, her lipstick breath overpowering me as she slicked my hair. I searched my face in the mirror.

My eyes, a shade not quite green, not quite gray, looked back at me over sags of flesh on top of broad cheekbones. My face and chin seemed in good shape, no lines around the mouth, a few laugh lines at the eyes and only a touch of gray in the hair. It was the eyes that scared me. Close up, the laugh lines turned to fissures and moats, with cracks and mesas of pouty bunched skin on the eyelid and above the bags of the cheekbones. The irises looked like miles of spring ice, glassy smooth on top, shot through with tiny fractures, ready to shatter at the slightest jolt, holding on by a fingernail for the warmth of spring. I was closer to forty than I liked, but these were thousand-yard eyes, a veteran of twenty-two with a sixty-year-old gaze.

When the hell had I acquired them?

"So?" said Irene, her hands on her hips. I patted the back of my head in hopes the cowlick was tamed. "Did you get any sleep?"

"A little."

"How little?"

"None, okay? Leave me alone."

"Did you get out of your clothes?"

"Who elected you mother?"

"What did you do then, when you were not shaving and not changing and not sleeping?"

"I drove around."

"You mean you slept in your car."

"Maybe."

"Did you or did you not spend the night in your car?"

I did. I really did. But I'd be damned if Irene was going to bully it out of me.

She took my arm and guided me over to the single club chair I used for required office reading. She pushed me down until my butt met the cushions. She lowered a thigh onto an arm and looked down at me.

"I know you got Christina out."

"So then what are you bothering me for?"

"Where did you sleep?"

"I parked out by Sea Cliff. I wanted to hear the waves. Usually it soothes me."

She nodded and got up. At my desk she turned around, rumbled out to her desk, and returned with a brush in her hand. She slapped it in her palm, like a cop wielding a nightstick in front of a bunch of gangbangers.

"I left her at the Ritz," I said.

"It's an awfully expensive hotel."

"She just got out of jail," I said. "She's the chief suspect."

"You wanted to bring her home?"

"She's alone. Joe's dead. Her family's not here. Most of her friends were Joe's."

"So you're supposed to take in your best friend's accused murderer? Do you have any idea what that looks like?"

"There's no way she did it. He was killed with a bat. She's maybe ninety-five pounds. She thinks getting messy is wearing jeans and a silk blouse."

"Give yourself a break."

"What are you talking about?"

"You know what I'm talking about."

"No, I don't."

"Oh, for God's sake," she said. And she walked back to her desk, sat down, and began banging things around like a chef angry at the help and taking it out on the pots and pans. I launched out of the chair.

"I do not know what you are talking about," I said, looking down at her now.

"Really?" she said, a scornful tilt to her head and downward curl in her lips.

"Really."

"Let's see. She dumped you for your best friend. Your rich best friend. Then best friend gives you all his business, gets your name in all the papers and your practice goes bananas and ya-ya and you're a sort of a gimcracking celebrity for the superrich, a lapdog who plays cute tricks and jokes, besides all the money you save them with generation-skipping trusts and estate tax gimmicks. And for the ten years since I started, you think you owe your buddy one, a big one. No matter what he did. And suddenly he turns up dead with your old girl in jail, and like the schmuck you are, you get her out, without a blue-sky thought what the cops will think or whether they'll ever find out you and Christina there were a number, a hot little ticket as they say. And you, you sorry-ass excuse for a man, thinking like a dick, feel *guilty* that you didn't let Christina sleep at your house last night!"

We stood looking at each other, she out of breath, me too stunned to suck air. Two prizefighters too weary to throw the next punch.

"Well" is all I could manage.

She got up again and walked over to me. I had to fight the

urge to back up. She took my hand and opened it to the palm and slapped her hairbrush into it. I would have said "ouch" if I hadn't been so shocked already.

"It's because you cut it yourself," she said, nodding at the back of my head.

"It's fine." I passed my hand over my head again.

"No, it's not. Go to a barber."

"And pay twenty-five bucks?"

"I pay a hundred."

"My point exactly."

"Get it fixed. Give him your first nickel. You're a rich guy."

"I am not rich."

"You save everything. Plus you get family money."

"My old man was rich."

"So. There you go. Just wait," she said. I paused a minute and looked at her. I kept my voice level, my face soft.

"He's been dead five years."

"I knew that. I did," she said.

"I know. There was no money left."

"Oh," she said, and then brightened. "Still, you make plenty. You're richer than me."

"I should be. I pay your salary," I said. "And I am not cheap."

"I know," she said. "Just thrifty." She went over to her desk and pulled out some old envelopes and personal stationery. They were yellowed and pale with an old address fading on the back flap. There was a post office forwarding symbol stamped on all of them.

"See, the post office forwards it," I said.

"Only because I pay them to. They only do it for free for the first year."

"Your loss then."

"Yours. I pay with an office check."

I took the brush and attacked the back of my head. The cowlick surrendered under the onslaught.

"Go get a haircut. I'll take care of Lewman's paperwork."

"I don't need one."

"Go," she said. "See what Mata Hari does."

Chapter 9

I didn't go to the barber, but I did go home for a shower and a shave and then drove back out to the bottom of Market and the wharf on the quiet bay. I bought a huge cup of coffee, made campfire style in a large aluminum pot at a wooden shack serving homemade sugar donuts. This side of the bay was still, with Oakland shining across the water and morning ferries heading for their downtown berths. Finally I got back in my car, twisted the key, and headed up California Street two blocks to collect Christina from the hotel.

The closer I got, the more I wanted to turn around. The more my resistance grew, the more my mood darkened. By the time I pulled up at the Ritz-Carlton's circle, carved out of an alleyway between huge office buildings and lined with niches of glass displaying jewelry and ten-thousand-dollar alligator purses,

I wanted to grab someone's larynx and squeeze. The morning checkout crunch had departed, and the bellboys stood around having a cigarette break. When I pulled into the circle in my Audi, they kept smoking.

I turned off the car, pocketed the keys, and made for the huge revolving doors, manned by another bellman inside whose job was to punch a button that ignited the motorized doors.

"Hey, you can't leave that there," said a bellman, detaching himself from his cigarette and stepping away from his smoking buddies.

"I'll only be a minute. I'm just picking up a guest."

"Still," he said, kicking a toe at the ground and looking at me with a blank pained expression. I took a step toward him, eyeing his throat.

"I don't want it moved."

"The city won't let us leave cars there."

"Tell them you didn't, I did."

"I need the keys," he said.

"So do I," I said, jingling them in my jacket pocket and walking inside.

When I stepped into the elevator, it accelerated so sharply that a hollow pit grew in my stomach where none was before. Reaching the fifty-sixth floor, nosebleed territory for an apartment or a hotel room, a sense of relief jettisoned me from the elegant box. It faded as I walked down the carpeted hallway toward Christina's room, caught in a swirl of black uneasiness, jangling nerves from too much coffee and a bubble of slow purple sadness, as if I were pallbearer at a friend's funeral and had not had time to say goodbye. At the door, I stood for a moment, waiting for it to subside, this strange, untidy cauldron, and prayed for my return to normalcy; my energy, my skeptical optimism, my ability to retain facts and numbers and above all to see clearly, objectively, factually. I waited for all this to return, but the door opened.

Her hair was wet and stringy, and the damp of it wafted over me.

"I thought you were breakfast," Christina said, wrapped in a short terrycloth robe that came only to midthigh. There were freckles in the V of her neck that I remembered matched a swatch on one of her shoulders I couldn't yet see. Her lips opened and spread in a wide lopsided grin, the teeth so white against skin with a tinge of brown. The light came out her eyes and fed on me and warmed me in a way that made me flower and stagger all at the same time.

"Come in," she said, opening both arms for a wide-open hug.

I melted into her embrace and the compact smallness of her, with both tenderness and fear for her safety. I had always wanted to protect her, even when I realized I needed to be protected from her as well. With her arms around me and the robe slightly parted but still belted closed, she spoke so closely I felt her breath trickle at my neck: "It's so good to see you today, Max. I'm feeling better, thanks to you. Now that I'm out of that awful . . . place."

Before I could answer, she let go and slid her hand in mine, her tiny hand, a thin, soft, electric touch, and led me down the short narrow hall into the wide suite.

"You got me a beautiful room," she said, letting me stand on the threshold and look out the large plate-glass window to the Bay Bridge and the Oakland Hills. Morning traffic streamed across the span and a Sausalito ferry cut a white wake to the Ferry Building docks directly below me. At this height, the three or four blocks across from the bay to the hotel seemed no longer than the length of a domino piece. "I feel like we used to," she said.

"It would be nice if it were true," I said.

She was no longer the wandering soul; when I met her, she was a refugee from a double-wide trailer girlhood. A childhood filled with dust belt farms and their bleached nightmares and petty horrors. Her father was a well-known rodeo TV commentator gone first to seed, then drunk, then bankrupt. Her mother, from a Midwest barefoot farm, ran off with a whiplash bronco rider to the Texas panhandle, then scuttled back when he left her at a rodeo. Mom settled into managing a hairdresser's shop in Little Rock and pushed Christina into majorette competitions. She had shown me a scar where her mom took a baton to her and broke her wrist in two places after she dropped a baton in competition.

She wasn't that girl anymore all right, as I looked at her in that elegant suite overlooking the bay while she told me she had put the room on her own credit card, not mine. A week ago it would have been Joe's.

"You know what I mean," she said, bowing her head.

There was a couch against the wall. She drew me toward it, and we sat down. She kept her hold on my hand and I couldn't keep standing. The cushions hissed a sigh. She snuggled into my shoulder. I sat as straight as I could muster.

"Christina. We should talk."

"Talk first? Sure. But you've changed," she said. "The Max I knew would never talk first."

"Funny, Christina. Very funny. We need to figure out some stuff."

"Yes, it's true. Things are an awful mess."

She wiggled closer to me on the couch and I could feel heat rise between my eyes and on the back of my neck. A hollow emptied out my belly, and I felt the hard flange of lust rise. I took a deliberate breath.

"Christina," I said, "we have to think."

"I know," she said, snuggling into me closer. "What should we think about?"

I couldn't see her face, but I could see the part in her hair and smell her scent and feel the tips of her fingers moving on the flat of my stomach.

"Christina. Look at me. Joe's dead. Guthrie thinks you did it. We can't just sit here and pretend nothing's happening and fuck."

She sat up a little straighter. "I know Joe's dead. He was my husband. Remember?"

"I remember," I said.

"Let's not bring up past horrors or old pain. There's enough for the present, don't you think?"

"Were you and Joe separated or not? He told me you were."

"When did he tell you that?"

"The night before he died. He said I had to help him. And then he said you guys had split."

"He wanted to talk about the investigation?"

"Yes."

"He was very worried. He was afraid you wouldn't help."

"Why?"

"You know why. You may have forgiven us, but you haven't forgotten a thing."

"How could I?"

"Even elephants forget . . . with time."

"Christina, were you separated or not?"

"So, Max the detective is on the case, hard at work."

"Christina."

"There's separated and there's separated. We were going through a rough time. I don't deny it. But I don't believe Joe wanted to divorce me. We wanted to adopt. It's a shame you never saw that part of him. He would have been a very good father, much more patient than I."

"Were you living there or not?"

She stood and left me on the couch and walked to the window. Next door, a new building was under construction. The latticework of scaffolding skinned the building while a crane on the roof dropped a cage of workers down the vertical glass. The muffled sounds of hammering intermittently entered the room, which provided a comfortable oasis of leisure and rest, while outside the world toiled through another workday. She looked outside, her back to me, arms crossed in front of her and her shoulders leaning inward. Sometimes I felt she thought she was in a remake of *The Maltese Falcon*, reprising the role of Brigid O'Shaughnessy. Then she'd slip on another character.

"You won't believe me," she said.

"Try, will you?"

"I was living there, but we were separated."

"How can you be separated and live in the same house?"

"For God's sake! Don't be so Victorian. This is San Francisco. This is where the cops go *home* to use handcuffs. We weren't sleeping together, okay? You want more details?"

"No. But do you expect anyone to believe that?"

"I don't care whether anybody believes that or not."

"You should. You're under investigation for Joe's murder."

"We weren't fucking! We weren't sleeping in the same bed. Is that enough?"

"No!" Then I asked, "Why not?"

She whirled around, the hem of her robe twirling open and revealing a flash of her thighs. They were thin and strong. The way I remembered them. And she was tough and light all at the same time.

"Why what? Why weren't we sleeping together or why weren't we fucking?"

She threw the last word at me, spreading it out, twisting the knife and watching my face for effect. I stayed calm. I willed blankness onto my face. I wondered how I would ever remove it.

"He kicked me out, okay? Does that make you feel better?" she said, looking down at the rug. She put her arm out for the desk chair and turned it around. She sat down. Her hands gripped the dark wooden back of the chair, and I saw the red lacquered fingernails glint.

"He didn't want me anymore," she said.

It was quiet in the room for a moment. Then the sounds of construction drifted through the windows again. Light strayed through the gauzy curtains. Dust motes wavered. A chill rose on my skin.

"I'm sorry," I said. That could have been a fatal blow to a woman like Christina. I was surprised she had revealed something she had never before experienced. Rejection.

Her hands untangled, and she looked up at me from her hunched-over position. "It had to be someone else. With his libido? Somebody rich without the wrinkles," she said.

"You don't have wrinkles."

"He had another woman. Otherwise he would not have thrown me out. He was always . . . a needy man that way."

"Do you know anything about his business?"

"Only that it's grown huge. He hated his old small-pie investors calling and complaining or demanding their money back. Wasting his time on pilot fish. He was always dealing with a crisis. Holding hands. Putting out little fires. He was very harried at the end."

"Really? Joe? Harried?"

"Yes. More than I had ever known."

"Okay. I'll check it out. After the funeral tomorrow."

I stood and went to the desk behind her to gather my jacket. She put a hand on my shoulder.

"May I come?"

"It's a very bad idea."

"I was his wife for five years, for Christ's sake!"

"It will make a scene if you go."

"It will make a scene if I don't go."

"Christina, everyone there will despise you for it."

"They despise me now. They despised me before. Does it matter?"

"Please." For some reason I could not explain, I did not have the energy to say goodbye to Joe and take care of Christina at the same time. It would suck me dry, leave me a black hole.

She searched my face for a long time, then said, "Okay, for you, Max, I won't go."

"Thank you. Just stay here, relax if you can, and I will call you tomorrow. Okay?"

"Yes, Max."

I went out the door in a breath of relief, guilty at escaping, my feet whisking down the hall as if the hounds of hell were behind me.

Chapter 10

Joe's funeral was on a day so clear, so breathtakingly beautiful that it made you wonder what kind of joker lived upstairs. The battered Romanesque church squatted off Highway 1 in Half Moon Bay, where a sargasso sea met fields of ordered green artichokes and a vaulted robin's egg blue sky. Mourners had gathered early, and there was a large crowd. Most of the people had driven down from the city and looked above them as they filed in, many staring at the rafters and unwashed stone with suspicion, as if the church hadn't decayed enough to achieve celestial dignity or scarred enough to achieve earthly wisdom.

The priest awaited the arrival of Joe's father. Paul Meaghan Dempsey, thin and spindly, dressed in a new three-piece black suit that would have made Joe proud, entered finally and sat hunch-shouldered and shrunken in the front pew. Pallbearers processed forward and placed the coffin before the altar. The service under way, the priest spoke eloquently but without passion or knowledge of Joe, the way an accomplished politician can deliver a well-rehearsed speech. He hit the touchstones of Joe's mother's early death and the solitude of Joe's and his father's life together in Albany, New York, where the tight-lipped senior Dempsey had been a firefighter, first on a truck-and-ladder crew and then as a driver and crew captain. Joe had brought him out to California when he hit it big and bought him a house on Half Moon Bay where the weather blustered and roared enough to remind the old man of upstate New York and its plentiful green fields.

When Paul Dempsey pulled himself to his feet and mounted the steps, the crowd deepened into silence; not even creaks from the pews fought for attention.

His black suit and white hair stood out from the vibrant blue of stained glass glowing behind him. He clutched the sides of the lectern with calloused palms. His voice throttled low, a truck rumbling downhill.

"Joe was smarter than me," he said. "And I knew this from when he was in third grade. He started his multiplication tables at dinner one night and I realized he was faster. He always won our debates, making a comeback to my simple points. He was faster, smarter, and taller than me, and we both knew it, thank God."

He looked down at his blunt-fingered hands.

"I've seen my share of death. Early death. Ugly death. I have learned enough faith to believe that there is some reason"—he looked at the priest, who nodded—"some good reason for all this, but it is hard. Hard to bear, hard to shoulder, harder to carry."

A slowly welling shroud of grief rolled forward as women

began weeping openly and men reached for handkerchiefs in vain attempts to stomp upon their own tears.

"But we must bear it. And we will bear it. And go on. For that is what the Lord commands." The sadness of the crowd rose like a wave as Joe's father was borne upon it.

"He was a good son. He bought me a house here in Half Moon Bay when I retired; or rather, when my knees retired, even though my desire did not." He stopped again and looked up at the crowd. A smile waxed near his face, a cloud passing over the moon on a windy night, but it was gone as he surveyed the upturned faces and the heaving shoulders shuddering throughout the crowd.

"He was a good son; I don't need to tell you that. He grew up while I was fighting fires, and then he grew past me, the way all children do." Paul Dempsey's voice descended another octave and ran out of register and stopped. Sniffles filled the church, and quiet sobs, held tight, reverberated off the rafters.

"I have seen enough of this, when men fell in the line of duty, to know what to do. And I always thought I was there to help the family through their loss. The young widows with children were the hardest, but we got them their husbands' pensions, and the first year we made a habit of babysitting for them. And it's only now I understand what we were doing. We weren't helping the widowed wives and kids. Oh, I guess we were, but we were helping ourselves much more. So today is a day where we grieve together, for grieving alone is a bitter thing that shrinks us up like fields of drought. But if we do this together, something passes through us, Joe himself passes through us, and we can feel both a little bigger and a little emptier. We can feel him go and know he is where he should be." Mr. Dempsey's chest heaved and he stopped.

Irene, beside me, wept, though she hadn't liked Joe at all.

Her black dress spotted with the wetness of tears falling on her lap. She gripped and kneaded her patent leather black purse with white-gloved hands. I pulled a handkerchief out of my breast pocket and gave it to her. She gave me a pat on the thigh and lowered her face into it, wiped her eyes, and surreptitiously blew her nose.

Paul Meaghan Dempsey held on to the lectern, fingers gripping and white, elbows supporting his weight, and looked out at us and spoke again, his voice an old, worn-out chisel rasping over newly rolled and minted steel. "We shall go out to the graveyard, all of us, and commit my son to the earth, and we will do it together, for that is the only way we can. Thank you for coming. For coming from your jobs and families, from far away, to help me see my boy off."

Mr. Dempsey stepped away from the lectern, not stooped, a light step down to the benches and the seated people who came out of their seats to lay their hands on him, touching the folds of his suit. Slowly, he shriveled and hunched over and began to weep on himself.

The sobbing crescendoed and the priest, standing now and still as an unlit candle, waited. He let the waves of sorrow gather and roll from throat to breast and back again. As it began to ebb from weariness, he took to the altar and straightened himself. I saw him speak Joe's name to the cross and send a prayer heavenward. The priest spread his hands wide, palms up, and the mourners rose, united, to watch as the coffin was carried out of the church, Joe leading us to his final destination.

The sun poured over the Santa Cruz mountains to the east. It was not late enough for the heat to build and unusual for Half Moon Bay to have no fog bank stretched across its coastline.

The graveyard lay on the edge of multiple artichoke fields that at a distance looked like symmetrical rows of four-leaf clovers.

Twenty yards beyond a circular drive lay an open grave covered with the false green of Astroturf. Joe's glossy wooden coffin lay supported by steel bars, the machinery to lower it obscured.

Not a breath of wind swept in from the sea. Irene threaded her arm through mine as we all approached the grave.

I saw Christina across the street from the cemetery, sitting in her idling Lexus on an access road, one that paralleled the sea and was nearly hidden by the rise of the land. Her car door opened and she joined a late group of mourners coming across the open field, a dark figure against the sea. Dressed head to toe in black, sheer black nylons, black flats, and an Audrey Hepburn hat with a veil underneath, she could have stepped out of *East of Eden*.

Christina pushed through a knot of people close to the grave, and when she stood at the edge, Paul Dempsey saw her and stiffened. The crowd stilled. Then Mr. Dempsey broke his gaze from her and I saw no anger in his face. He looked down. He was nodding to himself, as if discovering something he had known but never said out loud.

The priest, still in his purple vestments, opened a well-thumbed book of funeral rites draped with ribbon markers. He turned to a marked page and began, "I am the resurrection and the life." His voice held a new gust of rising wind, and the mourners quieted and slumped as they looked at the coffin. My mind drifted as I heard his voice and watched the breeze ruffle the hair of down-turned heads.

Christina's face was blocked by the wide brim of her hat, her head tilted down at the grave. There was none of the torrent of emotion that had built earlier; there was only sadness now, and frailty, as the priest finished his short prayer: "And we commit your son, Joseph, to you, our Lord, for keeping and safety." With a soft hum, the machinery lowered the coffin into the grave.

The priest knelt, took a handful of earth, and threw clods on the top of the coffin. Paul, knees bent, scooped both hands into the dark soil. He spread his full, cupped hands over the grave and then parted them and the dirt fell down, some dust spraying over the mourners so that a few turned their heads. Others took turns scooping and throwing dirt, and soon the file led away from the grave, through the cemetery to the access road where all the cars were parked.

I approached the open grave and the cherrywood coffin with the thudding of clods loud in my ear. I bent down and scooped two hands of the earth, dry with the spicy smell of peat and fertilizer, and spread my hands, and the earth fell loudly on his coffin.

Chapter 11

I walked alone across the fields and noticed two men standing near my car. One was a black man in a gray snap-brim hat and dark suit and the other a white man wearing jeans and a Hawaiian shirt and holding a tan jacket slung over his shoulder. They leaned against my Audi, and the white guy took out a pack of cigarettes and mouthed one. I could see his jet-black hair pulled into a ponytail when he bent over to light the cigarette. The black man turned his face to look at him, then languidly reached out a long arm and snapped the end off the cigarette. The filter stayed in the white guy's mouth. The black man put his arm down and cupped his hands in front of him like a schoolboy at the head of the class.

When I came near my car, they pushed themselves off my fender and stepped forward. Ponytail flicked his cigarette filter under my car. The black guy took his hat off, pulling it away from his head by the crown with two fingers. Ponytail reached around into his back pocket and pulled out a wallet.

"Mr. Smoller?" he asked.

I nodded. "Yeah."

He flipped open the wallet and I saw a silver badge inside. I was about to protest but realized I wouldn't know a real badge from one you could buy at a dollar store.

"I'm Arty Hannaford," he said, "with the San Francisco PD." He nodded at his partner. "This is Detective Hopkins."

I looked at Hopkins. "As in Lightnin'?"

"As in Napoleon."

"Napoleon?"

"Detective Napoleon Hopkins," he said and flipped open the badge carrier that he pulled from his breast pocket. He was a big man, with the gentleness of someone who had been big all his life. He held his arms across his chest and shrugged. "My mother was a history buff." I was about to ask him about his father, but Hannaford stepped in.

"Mr. Smoller, we caught the Dempsey case. We wanted to ask you a few questions about Joe."

Behind them, in the road, Christina's gold convertible glided by. She sat in front, both hands on the wheel, her face wrapped in large sunglasses and a scarf over her hair. Jackie O out for a Sunday drive.

"Mr. Smoller. A few questions?" Hannaford asked again, leaning in at me.

"Sure," I said, pulling my eyes off her car, "of course."

"You know Joe a long time?"

"Ten years. About. We met at Andersen. Arthur Andersen accounting, not the consulting side."

"You an accountant then?"

"Yeah."

"You do his taxes?"

"Yeah."

"Sign them?"

"Some. Until a couple of years ago. You can check yourself."

"Actually, we have to get them through the DA. Right now they're his wife's property."

"Oh."

They nodded. I watched Christina's car turn onto Route 1 from the cemetery and head north, up to the city. Gulls wheeled in front of us, and their raucous cawing mingled with the sunshine and the brine smell of the kelp beds from the sea.

"What about the DA?" I asked.

"Guthrie? He showed us what he took from the home."

"That's not enough?"

"He's running for mayor. Wants arrests, headlines. We were hoping you would give us something more than just obvious background information. Maybe your copies of his returns. Help us get to know her."

"Me?" I asked, pointing at myself and turning to see if someone else was standing behind. Hopkins shifted his weight to his other leg, and Hannaford tilted his head sideways a degree or two, like Alfalfa's spot-eyed dog, Pete the Pup.

I said, "This is where you ask me if I can give you stuff that you know I can't. And then you ask me, 'Don't you want to find who killed one of your best friends?' And I say, 'Sure.' Like I said sure before. But then I say—I really say—'I don't think she did it, and the files are technically hers, and I was the one who found her a lawyer, and I can't.' So that conversation's over."

They looked at each other and seemed impressed. Then they nodded at each other, too, and looked back at me.

"Cute," Napoleon said. "But we need to find a money trail."

"What is that? Like the Chisholm Trail? You going to lead cows across it?" I asked.

Napoleon Hopkins stepped forward, all six four of him. "Look, Max. He's your best friend. You just buried him." He stopped and pointed with a hitchhiker's thumb over his shoulder toward the grave.

Hannaford put a hand on his arm. They didn't make eye contact. Hannaford came up even with Hopkins. A wall in my face. "We caught you just after you buried your friend, and you're a little nervous. Maybe you get sarcastic when you're nervous. And you just got Christina out of jail. But you might want to think about this, because we're just trying to find a motive," he said.

"For God's sake! Guthrie's already convinced Christina did it. He already got the will. He's convinced she beat him with a bat before he could sign it. What more motive do you want?"

"You've known Christina a long time?"

"Yeah."

"How long?"

"Ten, twelve years."

"She strike you as dumb?"

"Sharper than a paper cut. Though you can't tell under that getup. But she doesn't miss a thing. Sees right through everybody. Except for men she's interested in; then she's blind as a duck flying over shotguns," I said, and added, "Lousy taste in men."

"Even Joe?"

Even Joe? Even me? The question ate through me like poison, like chemotherapy. I took a deep breath of air and thought about asking Hannaford for a cigarette, but I didn't want the shared bond between us. I turned and looked at him.

"It's hard to imagine Joe dead. You . . ." I swallowed, my

tongue dry in my mouth. "You didn't know him. As soon as he left the room everything went to black and white."

Hannaford took another step closer to me, nodding. "It's shocking."

I craned my neck back in surprise. "That was exactly it. Shocking."

"You know the way when you read a good book it seems more real than real life? Joe was like that," I said. "It's hard to believe it goes away when you close it." I could still hear clods thudding on the coffin. While the sun beat down on the distant artichoke fields.

"We see it, too," he said.

And I looked at him and saw a deep and sad knowledge in his face. He had seen it before, many times.

"We see it, too," he said again.

Hopkins stepped up to me and added, "Isn't there anything you can help us with?"

I asked, "Is it always the money? Is that all you guys do? Just follow the money?"

"Max," Hannaford said, "people don't kill for money, they . . ."

Hopkins finished, "They'll say they wanted forty bucks, or the season tickets to the Giants, or the boat on the Sacramento, or the keys to the business, or a zillion things that they make in this world."

This time Hannaford did take out his cigarettes. He toyed with the box, flipping it over like a dealer shuffling cards one-handed.

"But it's never really about the money," he said.

Hopkins gingerly put on his hat. "But it is the proximate cause."

"The delusion," Hannaford said.

"The delusion?" I asked.

"Illusion, delusion, whatever you want to call it," Hopkins said with a shrug.

"They can't live with emptiness," Hannaford finished, and now he tossed off a shrug too.

"What are you, a philosopher?" I asked Arty.

Hopkins rolled his eyes. "A Buddhist."

Hannaford glanced at his partner. He smiled. "Zen," he said. "It goes with the ponytail."

I wanted to help them, so I guess they had done their job. The good cop routine had worked, though there was a "but." With me, there's always a however, a whereas, an alternative minimum tax. Something that held me back.

"You guys don't think Christina did it?"

"Well, like you said, she's not dumb. The will was only a couple of days old, signed by Christina, not by him. The DA says you thought they were separated, but there's no evidence of that. She found the body and was covered in blood."

"It's not the profile of a money killer," Arty said. "They hire someone. Have an alibi."

"Motive's always the weak link," Napoleon said.

"You've got the will. She loses," I said.

"Too obvious. Doesn't add up."

"What about Guthrie? He sounds like he's going with what he's got."

"It's the smart play. The best odds. Good press."

"And you're not so smart?"

"Nope," said Arty. "Right, Nap?"

Napoleon rubbed his face. "We got a short window here. Before management yanks us off and closes the case."

"Management," I said.

"We're just hired muscle. Punch cards. Union dues," Arty

said, throwing a couple of air punches hunching behind a shoulder. "Coulda been a contender, Nappy could. Coulda been somebody."

"Art, give it a rest."

"Sure, Nap." Arty danced on his toes a couple of times, shrugging his shoulders, and touching his balled fists to his nose.

"Art."

"Okay, okay."

I watched all this, not knowing what to say. These guys were detectives?

"Listen, guys," I said. "I'll go over the stuff with you. But I don't think you'll find much."

"Why not?"

"I used to do his taxes; I know what's in them. They're pretty straightforward for a complicated business."

"You want to explain that?"

"Joe ran a hedge fund. He had a huge number of investments. Had a huge number of clients. But it's just sending out more 1040s or 1099s. Recording the income at the fund level was just a matter of keeping track of the trading. They divided it by the number of investors and their pro rata percentages. Not complicated. Just math."

"What's a hedge fund?"

"It's a private partnership that buys shorts and longs, distressed securities, derivatives to lay off risk, everything."

"This is simple?"

"Listen, why don't you guys come to the reception at his place? I'm sure there'll be a bunch of people there you can ask about Joe. A lot of his clients. I'll explain it to you then."

"I need a suit?" asked Arty.

"You don't own one," said Nap.

"Excuse me, Mr. Brioni."

Nap opened his jacket, holding the flaps open, and did a 360-degree pirouette.

"Ain't it grand?" he said, and out came this deep chuckle that rumbled into a delicious full-throated laugh. They turned and walked away, a pair of clowns returning to the dressing room after a second ovation.

"Five thirty," I shouted at their retreating backs.

Arty waved without looking back and opened the door for Nap. I watched them get in and drive away, making the same turn Christina had a long half hour before.

Chapter 12

Joe's Pacific Heights home was lit up stem to stern against a night fog bank. I stood on the white stone steps, which were not his steps or his house any longer, with the fog whipping across the top of the Heights and yellow lamps backlighting the walkway. The dark night and the cold took the heart out of me, and I wanted to turn around, to go home again. I had heard Joe eulogized and had thrown dirt on his coffin, but now, at this party, carrying his favorite whiskey through the doorway without him, a pall of sadness fell over me.

I had never grieved before, was unfamiliar with death in general, unaware of its river-flowing-by finality. A kid's toy got lost in the current, floating out of sight one moment, gone forever the next. I needed to escape but went inside. Having the reception at Joe's house had felt weird but Christina wanted it that way and made me pressure Guthrie to release the crime scene. She had the upstairs stains cleaned and the rugs thrown out. A metaphoric chin held high against her detractors.

I stepped through the oak front doors, flung open to the night, into the crowd of mourners eating, laughing, and smoking. Most were holding thick, multisided bistro glasses filled with wine and liquor. I passed an elegant gray-haired man in a brown suit and striped tie who said hello to me. I nodded back and took a deep breath. Looking right, where French doors overlooked the bright lights of Alcatraz and a black bay of night water, I saw a table loaded with wine, vodka, and already five empty bottles of Jameson. I put my fresh one next to them. A sixth stood half full until a man in a navy jacket and gray pants pointed at the bottle. The bartender poured him half a glass, but he tilted his head sideways, waving his hand, and the bartender filled it to the brim.

And so there was escape. I pointed at a new bottle and heard the cork pop, like a starving man hearing steak sizzle on a grill.

"Ah, now. Mr. Smoller," Danny Cleveland said. "Good to see you here. Sad days though. Very sad."

Danny bent his knees down to the table, stooped over, and with pursed lips slurped off the top of the full glass. He straightened up with a sigh of satisfaction and turned around with the glass in his plastic right hand.

"It is," I said. "Big party."

"Your hand is empty, sir. We must remedy that immediately." Danny Cleveland put out his good left hand and grabbed the open bottle of Jameson off the bar. "This is my wee private bottle," he said. If not for the broadening brogue, I wouldn't have guessed he had made the dent in the bottle's content by himself.

"I didn't expect you here," I said. "I think I owe you an apology."

"Nonsense, sir. Nonsense. I haven't the faintest clue what you are dithering on about."

"I haven't had time to call Armand Redfield."

"No apology need be considered."

"After you left my office, I went over to Joe's. The DA grabbed me from there. I haven't had a second to even catch my breath." My voice faded as my mind reeled from the fresh, scarred memory of the last three days. I rubbed my face to clear the movie replaying in my head. "Hard to believe, but it was only three days ago," I said, mainly to myself.

"Completely. I understand completely. Really I do, my dear boy. Utter shock. Utterly shocking."

He pursed his lips again and brought them down to the glass as if magnetized by a powerful force. When his face came away from the thick-walled glass, the glass was empty. He looked over my shoulder and stiffened suddenly. He placed a hand on my shoulder and looked at my face, his eyes wandering back and forth with drunken freedom.

"Nature calls, dear boy. Excuse me."

I watched him weave through to the kitchen, toward a bathroom I knew was off the butler's pantry. I took a drink of my scotch and felt its cool hot first sip. The one that always tasted good, never wrong. Knots in my shoulders and back loosened with the initial burn of it. Before I drank a second, the crowd parted quickly for another dark-suited man pushing through. I was slow to recognize him.

"Max," said Armand Redfield, "I'm glad you're here. I knew you would be."

I stiffened. "Armand Redfield," I said. "I can't say the same for you. What are you doing here?"

"I've known Joe almost as long as you."

"Not quite. Only if you call ten years—"

"I said almost, didn't I?" he interrupted. He kept on. "Max. This is a funeral reception. Can we just move on for a minute? I'd like to talk to you anyway."

"About what?"

"Who was that you were talking to before?"

"McClellan Cleveland," I said. If Armand already knew about Danny, I might as well go for it. It would be fast and easy, though possibly inappropriate at Joe's house. But if you don't use a hot iron, you never get the job done.

"Calls himself Danny," I said. "I was going to call you anyway. Look, all the guy wants is not to get his refund. I'm sure I don't know why. Maybe some divorce thing. He says he's not owed it. But can I come and talk to you about it? Show you his calculations, his 1040 maybe?"

"Who's Danny Cleveland?" Armand asked.

"You don't know?"

"Not from Adam. Weren't you talking to Michael Kessler on the way in?"

"I don't know Michael Kessler."

"Joe's silent partner. Michael Kessler. CleanEdge Technology Kessler? You were talking to him in the foyer."

"The blond guy when I walked in? That's Kessler? He's Joe's partner?"

"He just about owns the disk drive market."

"Bully for him."

"Joe was running half a billion dollars of his money."

"Half a billion? As in five hundred million?"

Armand smiled, pleased that finally I was impressed with him, or Joe, or both. "It adds up to real money after a while, doesn't it? Just a year's worth of interest for a guy like that."

"How much did Joe have under management?" I asked. Why I was asking Redfield I wasn't quite sure, but it was out of my mouth before I knew it. Sometimes, though, those are the best questions, the pop-out ones. I had honed my diplomatic interrogation skills trying to get under my clients' personal finances. It required the persistence of a detective and the subtlety of a card shark.

"Ten and a half billion dollars," Armand said.

"A couple of years ago I thought he only had a billion and a half."

"Joe did real well the past couple of years. Money was flying in from everywhere apparently."

"Apparently." I wondered why Joe had not told me. I knew his income was going up. His firm was growing. But not that big. Normally, he would have told me. Or maybe I just didn't listen.

"You talked to Joe about Cleveland?" I asked.

"No, of course not. You know the ethics rules better than anyone."

"What's that supposed to mean?"

"Nothing. I just wanted to meet Kessler. I've always admired the guy. Hero worship. You know." He turned his head and took a drink.

Then Redfield scuttled off. I saw him go over toward the bar and through a knot of people where I lost him as he threaded up steps leading to the entry foyer. When I went to replenish my Jameson a few minutes later, he was gone.

I ventured out to the foyer. Kessler was standing at the bar, his lean figure tilted at odd angles, an elbow on the bar, a hip stuck out. Behind him, Armand left the group, a look of fear tossed over his shoulder. I looked at my drink and swirled it around. The front door opened behind me and I felt the wet breath of fog on my neck. Compared to that cold draft, it felt good inside, with four walls around me, with the press of people and the smell of smoke and the clink of glasses and the hum of conversation.

Hannaford and Hopkins walked in with the fog, trailing the cold metal smell of it with them. They came up to me. Nap had his hand out, a big two-toned hand, the flesh of the palm pale white by comparison to the darkly shaded back.

"Max," he said, a smile stretching out his lips, his eyes looking beyond me to the crowd. Arty, in a tie, blue blazer, and a clean pair of khakis, came up and slung an arm over my shoulder, turning me to face the door. The two of them closed around me like bookends.

"Max," Arty said, "we ready to talk?"

"Sure," I said. "Sure. I was hoping to mingle a little bit first though."

"We really wanted to talk now."

"There're a couple of big shots I should get to first."

"We're big shots in your life now," said Nappy.

"The biggest," added Arty.

"I know. I know. Listen, I'll explain it all to you soon. Go over, get some free liquor. Tell everyone you played softball with Joe. You're friends. Firehouse 241, got it?"

"House 241. I think we can handle it."

I pushed through their shoulders and dove back into the crowd. Kessler had moved off the bar and was leaning into a different group of men and pearl-necked women who were nodding at him as he spoke, his chin pointed slightly up at the ceiling. Speaking over the crowd, to God presumably. Normally, I would have hesitated. Usually my distaste for crowds would have overcome me, but with Hannaford and Hopkins breathing down my neck, I pushed ahead.

"Mr. Kessler? Max Smoller," I said. His chin came down.

"*The* Max Smoller," he said. He knew my name, that got *my* chin up.

Then I said, "I'm Max Smoller." Again.

"You said that," he responded.

I had one of those moments, like when you're a kid at a new school and they're checking you out, sizing you up for the kickball team, the baseball team, the clique, the right table at lunch. You say something so stupendously stupid, so idiotic, it can't be taken back, erased, or ever forgotten. You carry it around forever.

He grinned wider. "I was wondering when you were coming over."

"How do you know me?"

"Joe talked of you many times."

"Really. Why?"

"The famous tax planner, fact checker, accountant extraordinaire."

"Me?"

"Does that surprise you?"

"All I did was the partnership accounts and the 1040s for the limited partners. Strictly routine. And I stopped doing that a couple of years ago."

"Joe relied on you more than you knew."

"Really?"

"Really."

I shrugged. "I only had to send in the W-2s."

"Minimize your role if you like." He stood up straight as he finished. I felt a hand on my shoulder. It stayed there as I turned around. Hannaford and Hopkins stood there, silly grins on their faces.

"Hey there, Max," said Arty, filling the quick silence as they pushed inside the little circle.

"We didn't see you at Joe's last game. How ya doin', man? Come on down to the firehouse and catch up. It's gonna suck without Joe. He was the softest touch, you know? Always giving me a fifty when the old lady was on my back 'cause I been drinkin' my paycheck, you know? Seems like we were just having a few beers at the 241 yesterday."

"I know," I interrupted, dreading this inane monologue.

Strangely, Kessler stepped forward. "I'm Michael Kessler. A friend of Joe's. We did a lot of business together."

"Arty Hannaford. This is my friend, Napoleon Hopkins."

"You guys firemen?"

"Working for the city, it's a gig, you know," Arty said. "Boy, Joe was a good guy; he could sit around on a Saturday afternoon and tell stories, man, stories. He was like our clown and campfire all rolled into one, know what I mean?"

"I suppose I do," said Kessler. "Let me introduce my friends." He stood aside and put out his arm, making way for a knot of men and women to step through and onto the stage.

"This is Arthur Molino. This is his lovely wife, Geena."

Arthur and Geena stepped forward to shake Arty's hand and say, "Hello," then moved on to Napoleon. Another woman stepped forward. She had on a long black dress with a high neckline, a small diamond at her throat. A white pinch around the flesh of her eyes and nose gave her a fearful, exposed expression. Her eyes were summer morning blue, and a pile of yellow hair stood on her head. She held a highball glass filled with amber liquor and ice.

"Ann Stoppard," she said. Then she turned around and offered up her husband, standing behind her. He stepped in, a tall wiry man with a mop of unruly graying curls, pushing forward, bent over like a question mark.

"Hi, I'm George Stoppard," he said. His high, reedy voice had the uncertain timbre of an adolescent boy. He coughed into his hand, then said, "Nice to meet you." His shoulders sagged and hunched, as if he were exhausted from all the wealth on his shoulders.

"Mr. Stoppard," said Arty.

"How'd you know Joe?" asked Napoleon.

Stoppard's eyes darted around the room seeking desperately to land on something solid and steady.

"Mr. Stoppard," Napoleon continued, "you do a lot of business with Joe?"

George Stoppard pumped a smile onto his face, which retraced the deep lines in his cheeks and mouth, like a statue smiling along tracks of dirt and grime. He looked at Nap a second, then darted his eyes back and forth between Nap and Arty. Ann looked up at him, a smile on her face, a political tableau.

"Not much," Stoppard said, "mainly neighbors."

Napoleon pushed on. "No derivatives? No mortgage trading? No futures? We heard Joe bragged he was making, what, forty, fifty percent a year. That true?"

"I was a small investor," he said.

George turned and handed his drink to his wife. Her corn silk bun caught the light on top of her head, turning it into a honey-colored torch. The single multicarat diamond pendant twinkled at her neck, held by a black satin band at her throat. How do the rich do it? She was so polished, elegant, poised. Does the sweet smell of success get under their skin and muscle, then make them glow like pregnant women, with a physical inner certainty, an *I am* shouted to a *you're not* world?

Ugly, awkward, rich men like George Stoppard always seemed to marry beautiful women. Wealthy men and gorgeous women were alike in many ways: a beautiful woman could never be sure she wasn't desired simply for her beautiful assets, and an ugly rich man could be sure he was.

"You sound like a policeman to me," George said, looking at Arty, still keeping that grimacing smile lining his face.

"Me? A cop? What makes you think so?"

"Well, first of all, the fire department code doesn't allow ponytails," he said, nodding at Arty.

He retrieved one of the highballs from his wife, drained it, and handed it back to her. He was flushed when he turned back to Arty and Nap.

"Second, no firemen wear Brioni suits from Wilkes Bashford. It's outside the culture, not to mention *way above* the pay scale. Same goes for the cops, except for the detective branch. If the homicide crew gets a lot of overtime, they can earn well into six figures. A couple of them even go for fancy suits. Plus, you've always gotten too much press, Detective Hopkins. And the owner of the *Chronicle* is a friend of mine."

"So, Mr. Stoppard," Nappy asked, a little smile on his face, "where do you get your suits?"

George smiled. He looked Nappy up and down. "Wilkes Bashford suits you good, Mr. Hopkins. You have the right shape. That enviable V. But me—a beanpole with a pouch for a belly? I tried a few at Wilkes. One or two off the rack at Neiman's, believe it or not. Finally, I had to go to Savile Row."

"Sharp," said Nap, studying Stoppard's dark green suit and bright canary-yellow tie.

"They end up being cheaper than Wilkes. And they do Prince Charles's suits."

"What's your tailor's name?"

"Anderson & Sheppard. They take forever. But you get a crotch that doesn't hang down like pajamas."

"Cheaper than Wilkes? Really?"

"I know what Wilkes sells Brioni for. They're cheaper. Believe me."

With a smile, Nappy asked, "Tell me, why does a man like you need to save a few bucks on English suits?"

George smiled back, twisting his mouth and bringing an

imaginary cigar to his lips. "How do you think a man like me gets to be a man like me?" His George Burns imitation was pretty good for a guy who stood six foot six and had real hair and no cigar.

The group broke up laughing. Arty, too. Tension whispered out of the room. People looked for drinks. George stepped up to Nappy.

"The chief's a friend of mine too."

"Lots of friends. That's nice."

"It is." Stoppard paused for a moment, then added, "I won't tell him you were here impersonating a fireman."

"That's nice, too. But you can tell him anything you want."

"I know you have to do your job. I'm glad you're doing it. But don't they already have Christina in jail for killing Joe?"

I stepped in. "She's out on bail, Mr. Stoppard."

"I see. The papers appeared to say it was open and shut. Why investigate?"

"Just doing our jobs," said Arty. Stoppard nodded.

He reached into an inner pocket of his jacket with long fingers ending in perfect half-moon cuticles and came out with a card.

Handing it to Arty, he said, "Give me a call. That's my private phone and e-mail. I'd be happy to assist."

"That's very kind of you, sir," said Arty. "We'll call if we need anything."

"We'll say goodnight then."

The group nodded to us and wandered off to the open part of the house. They leaned into each other, knowing this was a story they could retell a good dozen times at the next dinner party, the next performance of the ballet. The moment felt exciting, as if life was really alive.

Arty and Nap and I were left near the steps leading to the

front hallway, stranded and alone. The crowd had parted from us.

"Our cover's done," said Arty, surveying the party and guests.

Nap jerked his head at the door. "Come on."

Arty looked at me. "You got some 'splainin' to do, Lucy."

"Me? You guys blew the firehouse story before I could finish a drink."

"Stoppard's pretty smart. Rich, too."

"That's right," I said. "The old-fashioned kind." I smiled. "He inherited it."

Arty nodded. "So what the hell is a derivative?" he asked.

"Let's go outside," I said. "We need air for this."

I took them outside into the fog. It was cold even in our leather jackets. We got into their car, a blue Crown Vic with no hubcaps and three aerials sticking from the roof. It might as well have been a black-and-white. The seats could have been cleaned, at least once. Arty got into the driver's seat and promptly punched in the cigarette lighter.

"Man," said Nappy, "I thought you said you weren't gonna smoke and drive anymore."

"I ain't driving," said Arty around the cigarette in his teeth.

"At least turn the engine on so we can open the windows."

Arty twisted the ignition key and the engine turned over. The engine rumbled, exhaling O rings out of the tailpipe that the fog whipped away. Arty put the lighter back, puffing a filterless Camel. Eventually, he pressed his window button and the glass hummed downward.

"So what the fuck is a derivative?" asked Nappy.

I said, "It's pretty simple really. A derivative is a synthetic credit instrument that large institutions like banks or financial companies use to allocate risk to different companies or institutions over different time periods."

"It'd be pretty simple if you'd speak English," said Arty, nodding outside. "That's clear as this pea soup."

Nappy joined in. "You mean it's like insurance?"

"Exactly. Except with derivatives there's no payment on death or anything like that. One party is indemnified against losses, the other pays some negotiated amount. The only trick is that it's all based on credit."

Their eyes began to glaze over, so I took a breath and said, "Think of it like a poker game. The stakes are ten-dollar ante. Hands are going upwards of a thousand bucks. You only have fifty grand with you, five hundred in the bank. You make a deal with some guy who's watching the game, maybe the pit boss, maybe the house, that no matter what happens in the game, you won't lose more than ten grand. You lose more, they pay the difference."

"How much?"

"It's negotiable."

"Some negotiation," said Nappy. "Why would they bet on me?"

"It's not a bet. They're doing the same thing for the other players."

"Both ways?" asked Arty.

"Both ways," I said.

"That's pretty neat," said Nappy. "If I lose, they pay, but they got another guy on the other side of the trade, who pays them. They can't lose. That's a pretty good deal."

"It can be."

"That's not gambling," Arty said.

"No. It's business. They're in it to make money. That's why they call it business," I said.

"But they're just ripping people off, aren't they?" Arty asked.

I shrugged. "Nappy here paid him of his own free will."

"Because he couldn't take the risk."

"That's right. But he wanted to play."

"I guess so," said Arty.

"Still. It seems squirrelly to me. I work my ass off fifty hours a week, I'm making a grand after taxes."

"They're providing a service. People ask for it and pay for it," I said.

Arty said, "But . . ."

Nappy stopped him with a hand. "Arty. You happen to recall we're detectives? Can we just forget the social justice implications and find out what Joe did and why someone wanted him dead? We're supposed to be detecting."

"Jeez," said Arty. "What are you so touchy for?"

"Look," I said. "Joe did do some of this stuff. He bought stocks. Sold short. Bought derivatives, mortgages, high-yield debt. Bank loans. Pretty much anything."

I held up my hand when Arty started to ask more. Nappy rolled his eyes. Arty lit another cigarette, blowing smoke out of the side of his mouth while Nappy tried melding with the door. "He did lots of speculative trades. But it was all to make his clients money. Trading. Making different bets on different markets, or differential securities, the same securities—it's called arbitrage."

"There's no sense in that," said Arty.

"There's no motive in that," said Nap.

"That's what I'm telling you," I said. "He was just trading."

The conversation broke off and stalled; then Arty opened his door. The car was wrapped in a cocoon of gray as cool night air blasted through the opening. Arty got out and leaned against the front fender. He twisted his neck a couple of times, cracked his knuckles, looked at his fingers. Then he straightened and exhaled. He turned into the car and stuck his head through the window.

"Want a ride home?" Arty asked, looking at me in back.

"I live close."

"You in the high-rent district too?"

"Not this high. I live down in the flats. The Marina."

"It's nice," said Nappy, nodding.

"Not this kinda nice," said Arty, his head twisting and looking at the gargantuan houses guarding the spine of the Heights.

There was a fortress-like solidity to the houses. They gave the illusion time could not assail them, though it would. It was just that stone and cement and wood decayed slower than flesh. But a wrecking ball could destroy almost anything. So could a baseball bat.

"I'm going back in," I said. I pushed my door open.

"Brave soul," said Arty.

He pulled his door shut as I stepped out from the backseat. The light reflected off the window, and they became invisible as the car slipped away into the fog.

I climbed the steps again and opened the doors and was assaulted by the noise and the light and the heat, which hit me like a wake-up slap from a twilight sleep. I walked through the house, looking at Joe's pictures in the hallway, looking for Kessler or Redfield or Cleveland, anybody to talk to. There was no way Joe could have gotten that big without my knowing. He would have told me, if only to make sure I knew.

I scanned the place, walked to the fireplace mantel, and fingered the frames of photographs. A shot of JFK's hands reaching down to an adoring crowd. The house was peopled with a drunken band of firemen, the real ones from Firehouse 241, where Joe had left them with a trail of stories building into legend and drinking legends fading into history. Joe would be remembered at Uncle Tom's Tavern in the Bermuda Triangle, the trio of famed bars kitty-corner from each other on Fillmore and

Greenwich. Firemen launched into bad renditions of "Danny Boy" with full-throated toasts and tears dripping off stubbled cheeks, wiped away with fast, angry palms that stretched the skin of their faces. Toasts and tears drenched with Jameson.

I wandered back out the door and walked jerkily on the sidewalk like an untethered balloon. Before I got to my car, I realized I still had one of Joe's photographs in my hand. It was one of us at Andersen, back in the cubicle days. I hiked back up the steps, through the emptying house, now with quiet singing still in it, and replaced the picture on its perch. Joe and I, ten years ago, a lifetime younger, stood draped over our contiguous stalls at Andersen's old office south of Market. Joe was holding up our exam certificates, that easy contagious grin on his face, my own smile a haphazard reflection of his, lit not so much by our passage into certified public accountants as by Joe's virulent and happy ease, his comfort, his blarney.

We had walked through the labyrinth together and found the center of the maze. But we had not thought to leave crumbs for the trail back out. Why bother? We were so sure we could find it anytime. Joe's wandering was over for good now. And I had an empty path ahead.

I placed the photograph facedown and fled to the street. I started to open my car door, but a cloud of drink and gloom hung over me so I padded home through the fog. Once there, it only took a couple fingers more of single malt to fall downward into sleep.

Chapter 13

Morning broke with no easing of the previous night's heavy fog. From my small two-bedroom stucco, which the previous owner had trimmed in magenta, I looked through my view alley to the bay. No accountant is without a calculator when it comes to real estate, and if I ever sold the place, the alley was gold. I could see white froth on top of slate-gray swells and a tanker lumbering under the bridge out to blue water. Even at this distance, the tanker dwarfed the sailboats tied up a half mile closer at the docks; they looked like children's toys tethered in the bathtub by an orderly, compulsive parent.

The tang of cold and sea mist chilled the tile on my bathroom floor as I shaved. I took a steaming shower. I opened the door when I heard the phone ring. I paused, then stepped back into the shower and pretended I didn't know who it was.

I tried to push it out of my mind, but every jangle of the water gurgling down the drain sounded like a summons to another ringing bell.

I turned the water off, got out, and marched over to the phone as I dripped on the floor. I punched in Christina's hotel number, which I had written down on the pad beside the phone four days earlier. The operator answered, chirping, "Ritz-Carlton," with an Asian accent.

"Christina Lawson's room, please."

Background music. Clicks of a computer keyboard. A breath. "Sorry. No one here. No Ms. Lawson."

"Christina Dempsey, then."

"No Ms. Dempsey."

"She was there yesterday."

"No Ms. Lawson, no Dempsey. Thank you. Can I help with anything else, sir?"

"No, thank you," I said and put the phone back on the cradle.

Christina was in one of her moods again. She might pace the beach at Stinson for two days straight. Walk across the Golden Gate Bridge to Sausalito with a backpack and sleep in one of the World War II bunkers on Fort Baker overlooking the bay. Fly to Costa Rica and back. Shop in Hong Kong. Now I would have to go find her. Drive all over town. Call everyone. Leaving a trail with my name on it.

I pulled on a pair of pants and felt the dampness on the back of my knees stick to the khaki. I tugged. I heard a seam on the right hip rip. Fuck. I pulled out a sport shirt and yanked it on. A button popped. It bounced across my bedroom's wood floor. Goddamn Christina. I smashed my feet into some Top-Siders, grabbed my black leather jacket, and swept my wallet and keys off the kitchen counter under the kitchen phone.

I yanked open the door and froze. There was a small figure hugging its knees on my steps. A suitcase and an arm lay against the steel and wrought-iron railings. Christina turned and looked up at me from under her lashes, an "I dare you" expression on her face but a glint of fear behind her eyes. After she looked at me a second, the brave face softened, and she smiled and got up, grabbing leather handles.

"I'm here, Max."

"So I see."

"Aren't you going to invite me in?"

I shut the door behind me. She deflated a bit and leaned against the railing.

"Please, Max?"

"We went over this at the Ritz."

"No, *we* didn't. You talked. I listened."

"Didn't you hear anything I said?"

"Of course I did. I just didn't agree with any of it." She had eased up the steps to the landing and was now on equal footing with me. Her left eye fluttered as she put a hand on my arm.

Even now, her skin was flawless and had the gleam and glow that you only see in airbrushed magazine photographs. There were no flecks in her green irises now, and her breath smelled of mint, and her skin shone from the almond oil she used. It gave her the faint suggestion of India, of bongs and collegiate incense. But this wasn't a dorm room, and we weren't in college. This school was permanent.

"Christina, I explained it to you. If they see you here, Guthrie's going to have more of an apparent motive than he does already. Right now they have only one, not more, and a working theory, but you have two cops who believe you. Let's not screw that up."

"Who are they?"

"Two detectives."

"Their names?"

"Hannaford and Hopkins. They're the only guys on our side right now."

"Our side? I'm the one they're trying to pin a murder on." I sighed.

She said, "I just want to come inside."

As usual, she won. I picked up her suitcase and turned with it to the door. As I pushed the front door open for her, she smiled at me and took a little jiggle step over the threshold.

I was about to follow her inside when I heard the muttering purr of an engine and tires crackling against asphalt. I turned around as a Bentley coupe rolled to a stop at the bottom of my steps. Even in the morning mist, it shone like a dark green emerald. The front window whispered down.

George Stoppard's gray curls stuck out from the car's sill, and a jacketed elbow protruded. The folds in his face looked deeper than when I had seen him last. His dark eyes darted around the façade of my house before settling on me navigating down the stairs. He pointed his chin a couple of times at me. Michael Kessler sat next to him. His blond head nodded once, and a hand came up in acknowledgment.

"Good morning, Max," Kessler said.

"Going away?" Stoppard asked. I looked down, realizing I still had Christina's bag in my hand. Fortunately it was a leather duffel, something I could pass off as my own. I gave a quick glance over my shoulder to check that she was out of sight. Stoppard hadn't seen anyone.

"No. Just to the gym."

"Fancy gym bag."

"Fancy car," I said.

"You like it? Get in. I'll drop you off at your gym."

"Unless you want to wait at the curb like a chauffer, I need my own car to get back. Plus, the backseat doesn't look too comfortable for adults."

"You'd be surprised. I'll take you for a spin. You ever been in a Bentley before?"

"No."

He said, "Me neither. Get in." I dropped the bag back at the top of the stairs, stepped down, and circled the front of the Bentley Continental. It said right on the hood: "Bentley." I brushed a finger over the raised sterling badge. I opened the door, which felt as heavy as the door of a bank vault and swung shut as gently. Kessler leaned forward, and the seat tilted, revealing comfortable backseats for a sports car. Inside, the perfume of new buttery leather enveloped the cabin. It was so thick I could almost feel it coagulate on my skin and enter my pores, as if the sheen of wealth could pervade my entire body, organs and all.

"Whose car is it, then?"

"Test drive," said Stoppard.

"They let you just take it? Alone?"

He looked over at me from a slight old-man hunch at the wheel. His hands released and he sat back. I could see the backs of their heads as they just stared ahead. Waiting. Well, I could wait too.

"They let me take the damn thing for a ride. Silly really. People always think the rich are more trustworthy."

"They're not?" I asked.

"You should know," Stoppard said. "You see more of people's financial underwear than practically anybody, right?"

"You make me sound like some pervert."

"Not at all. An expert actually. How many times have you found people taking deductions they know they can't?"

I shrugged. "People love freebies."

"It's human nature to cheat the IRS," Kessler said to the windshield, his voice edging higher than Stoppard's.

"I wouldn't go that far. A very high proportion pay voluntarily. In general, people know what's a deduction, what's not."

"And those that don't?" Kessler asked.

"I try to show them the error of their ways."

I looked around. We were still motionless. The motor's idle was so quiet and the defroster so subtle I thought I was waiting for afternoon tea.

"Are you going to drive this thing?" I said.

"Certainly, sir," Stoppard said, playing chauffeur. "Where shall I take you?"

"It's your car," I said.

He slipped the car into gear and it muttered away from the curb. As he sidled into traffic without looking, a taxi honked behind him. A tap on the accelerator and the car showed its muscle under all that elegant wood and leather.

"So all your clients are as honest as the day is long, my friend?" Stoppard said.

"Why don't you guys just tell me why you're here?"

Stoppard looked over at Kessler, who twisted in his seat. He trained that patrician face and gray eyes under the blond hair on me.

"Joe wanted to go big in the fund business a couple of years ago and invited me in."

I nodded, hoping Kessler would just talk.

"He invited me in," Kessler continued, "because he wanted scale and size, which matters, that sort of thing."

"And why you?"

"Well, he knew of me. I was a small investor with him already, just trying him out. He asked me to take a piece of the firm in exchange for bringing in other larger investors and the capital for getting a track record to sell to others. Like my friend George."

Stoppard nodded. "It was all disclosed. Michael here put up a hundred million seed capital for Joe's short-long derivative funds, the risky trading, that sort of thing. After a year they had a track record, and I came in for a bit more. Just as a limited partner, an investor only."

Kessler nodded a look at me. "That's how things work. I took a risk." He turned forward as Stoppard eased the car around a corner. "And got paid for it. At Joe's request," he said, "I promise you."

I had no trouble believing it; that was Joe all the way. Give someone a piece of the pie and attract others in the right circle around them. I just didn't understand why Kessler had done it or why Joe hadn't tried to do it with Stoppard first. Maybe he had asked and gotten turned down.

Stoppard interrupted my thoughts. "I put up some money after Michael and Joe proved they could make money with their derivatives strategy. It was innovative, more creative than what my managers were doing for me."

This was the ceaseless churning, the restless course of the money river seeking more—always more—like water racing downhill, scoring canyons through rock.

"And you're telling me this because . . . ?" I asked, my voice ending a little higher than I would have liked. Kessler turned to the front, his part over.

"We're telling you this so you know there was nothing going on with Joe and us. George was simply an investor like any other, albeit the biggest one, but only that. I was a silent partner who introduced him to our friends and got a piece of the firm for making a bet on him."

"And . . ."

"We know you got Christina out of jail. We know Lewman. His MO is to find someone else to attack. We're telling you, we're innocent; we're not targets for you at all, and you better get your facts straight about that ex-wife of his."

"They weren't divorced," I said. "I know that much."

"Getting there fast," Stoppard said. "They had knock-down-drag-outs in the office, on the street, at Whole Foods. Anywhere."

"That right?" I asked. "How many people saw this?"

"Everybody," George said.

"She is a very nasty woman," Kessler said. "Made Joe's life a living hell. She screamed at office workers, secretaries—sorry—administrative assistants, reamed out the contractors at the house they were building. Anyone and everyone."

"They were building a house?"

"Just down the street from me," said George. "Bigger than mine. Swimming pool, squash court. Beverly Hills Pink." His cheek dimpled into a frown.

"Style did not fit in," Kessler ended.

"With you?" I asked.

"With the street's."

"He paid twenty million just for the lot," said Kessler. "Three years into construction and they're only half finished."

What was wrong with their old house? I wondered. The old one was five times the size of mine. The car made the last corner before my place. It stopped. George finally turned around himself.

"Look. We're not trying to tell you what to do. Defend Christina all you want. Joe was never quiet about your history together." *Great*, I thought, *fodder for the rich folks' snickering.* "But don't use us as a distraction."

"And don't go dredging up any of this hedge fund hysteria. There's nothing there. Christina couldn't have gotten any of it, and our financial affairs should not be public."

Kessler had turned around now too and they both looked at me. I was the little kid who had peed on the backseat and both parents were lecturing. George turned back and eased off the brake and we slid forward to my house.

The Bentley rolled to a stop at my steps. Kessler opened the door and got out, pulling the seat forward to let me out. I ducked my head out and stood up, coming close to his chest, face-to-face, his erect, thin body wrapped in rich, soft fabric. I looked into his eyes, gray and observant, but with a hint of black on the rim.

"Max, we all know you have a good reputation. Smart. Tough. Honest," he said. "Stay that way and stay clear of us. We'll all be better off. In the future especially. We won't forget. I promise," he said, putting out a hand.

Rather then take it, I pulled the seat back and looked under the roofline through the open door. "Goodbye, Mr. Stoppard. Thanks for the ride."

I stood up and nodded at Kessler, whose right hand had retreated into his jacket pocket. I walked around the back of the car and stopped at the bottom of the stairs. I turned, but the Bentley was already purring away.

The steps behind me seemed steeper then usual, and my legs labored up them. It wasn't until my hand hit the doorknob that I saw Christina's bag against the railing and remembered she was inside. Christ.

I opened the door slowly, determined to send her back to the hotel or to rent her an apartment somewhere.

Inside, I saw a shoe of hers lying on the entryway floor. She was already messing up the house. I followed it into the living room, the blue glow of my video system dappling the floor, expecting to see her in her favorite position, lying sideways, head on a pillow, watching a movie. Christina lay across the couch all right, but she was breathing laboriously, her right eye open, fixed and dilated, her left eyelid completely closed. Blood trickled from her left ear, tracking down across her jaw and beginning to collect in the fold of her shirt, spreading into a stain. I glanced around for another intruder, another bat. It couldn't happen again, Jesus.

"Christina," I said, putting a hand to her. "Christina." The right eye rolled back into her head and all I saw was white, a doll gone mad. There was no external damage I could see. I ran to the phone and punched in 911, barely finding the voice to describe her condition. The paramedics screamed up to the door a long six minutes later.

Chapter 14

The ICU at UCSF hospital was a fearsome place. Bodies lay inert in beds, tubes protruding from mouths, wired arms, all leading to machines, as if the fading vitality of flesh fed the machines that beeped in glowing life. I had spent a day and a night there on a hard chair in an anteroom, dozing every three hours after the doctors' rounds until finally, at five, the surgeon had woken me and handed me steaming black coffee in a mug stamped with I LOST MY ♥ IN SAN FRANCISCO on the side. When I held the mug up to read it, he grimaced at the macabre joke.

"I'm Dr. Macintyre," he said.

"How is she?"

"Stable," he said. I looked across the nurses' station to monitors that collected patients' oxygen and heart rates, the room filled with buzzes and drips. Low moans escaped from patients half awake or half dead while the steady beat of Christina's ventilator percussed the corridor's air like a snare drum.

Christina lay on her back in the bed of ICU #10, the intubation tube taped from chin to ear, protruding from the slack of her mouth. Her paper-thin gown had slipped off her shoulder, and there was no one to cover her up.

I walked in and pulled the gown over her shoulder as a doctor followed me in carrying a chart. Christina's skin was slack, and raw lesions dotted the backs of her hands and insides of her arms where they had inserted needles and tubes. Her left eye was still closed, the right one open, sightless. He put a hand on me and turned me toward the door but stopped at the threshold.

"How is she?" I asked again. "What happened?"

"We're still not sure. We ran an MRI and tests last night. We'll get preliminary reports this morning."

"The blood in her ear. Was it a stroke?"

"It's possible. Though her brain function is adequate. She's being sedated. She fought the ventilator briefly when we intubated her."

"You don't have a preliminary diagnosis?"

"Has your friend had any problems before this?"

"I don't know."

"What about her relatives. Who should we contact?"

"I told the admitting nurse last night. She only has a mother back in Texas, I think. Last I heard, she was in a nursing home, or ill; I can't remember. I don't know of anyone else."

"There won't be someone else to sign releases and insurance information?"

"I gave the nurse her wallet last night. She must be covered."

"Her insurance isn't the problem. We'd prefer a relative to sign."

He paused, then said, "No siblings?"

"No."

"Can you sign?"

"I have no legal standing."

"You'll have to sign as a temporary guardian." He handed me a clipboard with ten pages of legalese and bold printed exculpatory releases for the hospital. I flipped to the back page and signed.

"You'll need to initial every page."

"Why?"

"It's our procedure. She may need surgery."

"Now?"

"Possibly. Probably when the results come in."

"Why? You must know something."

"I'd rather not say."

"Look, Dr. Macintyre. I can't sign without some idea," I said, as I scanned down each page, flipping them over and glancing up at him as I spoke. He was a solid man, with black hair receding from a broad forehead, slight stubble on his cheeks from an overnight shift, and a hangdog look to his brown eyes from the deep and ineradicable pouches underneath. His hands were strong, palms meaty, the fingers thin with clean, well-clipped nails. He took the clipboard from me and put it under his arm.

"This is preliminary, you understand?"

"I do."

"It may change, depending on the test results."

"Doctor, just tell me. Did she have a stroke?"

"We don't think so. The bleeding from her ear was probably not serious. Most likely a punctured eardrum. It's unusual, though, in an adult; the membranes are stronger than children's, and usually it occurs through some accident, some trauma to the head."

"Did she fall?"

"There's no evidence of a concussion. But she may have fallen. We can't tell."

"So what's the problem?"

"Based on preliminary X-rays and MRI results . . ." He stopped. "This is before the radiologist has interpreted the MRI. You understand? I'm not giving you a diagnosis."

"Yes. Yes. Go on."

"There appears to be an archaic mass between her optic nerve and the ear canal. It's relatively large. Has she had symptoms before this? Shaking hands? Reduced eyesight? Dizziness?"

"I don't know."

"Any abnormalities at all?"

"I don't know. Archaic mass? What does that mean?"

"How much time have you spent with her lately?"

"Not much."

"How well do you know her? The nurse said you told her you were close."

"We were. I . . . we hadn't seen much of each other recently."

"How recently?"

"Look, Doctor. Can you just tell me what's going on? Without the third degree?"

"The mass is large, larger than I would have suspected in someone with no symptoms. There's no sign of hematoma, or other . . ."

"Doc," I interrupted. "Speak English. What is wrong with her?"

"Based on what I know—and that's very little at this point . . ."

"I know."

"I think she has a growth in her left occipital lobe." He paused and looked at his hands, then turned them over. "Sorry," he said and took a deep breath. "She has a tumor in the left side of her brain; it seems to be between her optic nerve and the ear canal."

"But, Doctor. Those. That. They're not that close. I don't understand."

"I'm afraid it's quite large."

"Large as in . . .?" I couldn't finish. How do you imagine the size of a tumor in someone's brain?

"It's about the size of a baseball."

"A baseball?"

"Maybe as large as your fist."

"Is that possible?"

"It's possible."

"With no symptoms?" I was about to ask another question, but a muffled rumbling began behind us. First there was the steady murmur of nurses quieting an agitated male baritone. Then the volume escalated until finally we both heard the loud man's words.

"Where the hell is she?" Footsteps came up behind us as we turned around.

"Is this her?" the man asked. He was young and buffed, facial skin the color of new olives, forearms a shade deeper. Black, oily hair and blue eyes. He wore an orange sport shirt that hung out over his jeans.

"Is that her?" he asked again, as he looked at Christina in the bed. His tan faded under the whitening face. The ventilator was loud in the room while he looked at her.

Dr. Macintyre stepped forward into the door, blocking his way. He was a shorter man and he had to peer up at Macintyre. I could tell he didn't like it. "Who are you?" Macintyre asked.

"Is that Christina?" the man asked, much more quietly, a crack in the voice gurgling at the end.

"That's Christina Lawson. I must ask you again. Who are you? I need some ID."

The man kept looking at Christina. "I'm her fiancé," he said. Something made the small, thin man turn around. He looked at Macintyre.

"Her fiancé?" Dr. Macintyre asked.

The man took a step toward the doc, invading that unmarked boundary all of us desperately seek to maintain. The doctor's cheekbones moved closer to his eyes a notch and there was a twist to his mouth that could have been a smile. He slouched against the doorjamb, put his shoulder on the sill, and crossed his arms in front of him. He was unruffled. Down the hall several different-toned beeps began. Nurses pattered down the hall to silence them. Christina's ventilator heaved and hissed.

"Then you won't mind telling us who you are. You can sign the papers I was just showing Mr. Smoller here."

"What papers?"

"Your name?" said the doctor.

"What papers?"

"I can't very well divulge confidential information to a stranger off the street, can I?"

They were quite close, and the small man could not budge the doctor's large mass, the beefy forearms crossed across a spreading stomach. Macintyre just watched.

"I'm Joe Arbeddo," the man said. "We were engaged." Another Joe? No way would Christina be such a cliché. That alone would rule him out.

"Were?"

"Are. We are engaged." He put out his hand to the doctor.

Macintyre shook it. He said, "This is Max Smoller. He brought her in."

Joe Arbeddo pushed out his hand to me. There was a deep scratch on the back of it, and the palm had two hard, raised calluses, one at the base of the thumb and another on the heel.

The fingers and joints had ridges with taut skin as well. It was a hardworking hand.

"That was nice of you," he said.

"Least I could do."

"Mr. Arbeddo," Doctor Macintyre asked, "you got a wallet on you?"

"Sure. But I don't have much money on me."

"ID is what I'm after," said the doc.

"Sure," he said, "sure."

Joe Arbeddo opened a buffalo wallet, faded and embossed with ridges and a brass buffalo nickel embedded in it. He opened it up. Credit cards were on one side, on the other a flap with a faded picture of a girl with braces grinning frankly at the camera in a blue sweater and plaid argyle shirt. The child had multicolored glass hanging at her neck between braids of reddish-brown hair. Clearly divorced or he'd have more recent photos. He slipped out a California driver's license. Macintyre took it and gave it a quick glance, moved his lips for half a second, then gave it back.

"Thanks, Joe," he said, then turned and grabbed the sheaf of papers and pushed them at Arbeddo. He had no choice but to take it like a football handoff during a broken play.

"Go on over there," Macintyre said, pointing his eyes at the nurses' reception and a barren chair and table. "Even if you don't want to sign, you should look at them."

Joe took the handoff and walked off, looking down at the papers, then shot a last glance over his shoulder at us. A nurse nodded him into a chair.

Macintyre turned his back and took out a pen. He turned his palm over and wrote something on it. Surprise must have showed on my face.

"His license number."

He looked at me for a second. "Med school trick," he said. "Photographic memory?"

"No. A type of mnemonics. I watch myself write it down in my head. It'll stay there for a couple of days. Then it will fade like something in Harry Potter's magic book."

"I'll have to try that sometime. I get phone numbers stuck in my head for weeks. But damned if I can remember my mother's best friend when I come to meet her again."

"You think you'll forget Arbeddo over there?" he asked, nodding to the dark head hunkering over the sheaf of papers.

"Not likely," I said.

"I didn't think so," he said. He took out his hand again and rubbed at the palm where he wrote the number down. "I'll get my assistant to call and check it." He rubbed it once more, then looked up at me. The brown eyes rested on me and I started to fidget a bit.

"What?" I asked.

"Did you know?"

"What?"

"She was engaged."

"I thought she was living with Joe."

"Another Joe?"

"Joe Dempsey. I buried him yesterday."

"I see," he said and looked at his hand. He rubbed at it again, even though there was nothing left but a smudge.

"Who is this Joe?"

"No clue."

"You never heard of him?"

"Nope."

"Is it possible?"

"That she was engaged to him? He doesn't seem the type."

"Meaning?"

"Christina liked more substantial men. Movers. Shakers."

I was neither, of course, just a modern scribe, a dusty, pale accountant, recording the gold strikes, the buried treasure and the secrets, the hidden things that the money trail left in its wake. You could follow that path through the maze, but never would I have the secret code for the hidden door, or the string to follow home.

"I see," the doctor said. My gaze swept up to his face and searched it. I didn't see anything in particular, but I couldn't hold his eyes. Arbeddo walked up behind us, waving the stack of papers in his hand.

"This stuff," he said, flipping it back and forth making the pages riffle in the air. "What is it? What does it mean?"

"It's just a power of attorney," said Macintyre. "It lets me operate if I need to."

"She needs an operation?"

"We don't know."

"What kind?"

"Mr. Arbeddo, this is awkward, but I have to ask. Do you have any evidence of your engagement? A ring? Anything?"

Arbeddo flushed under the V of his shirt, and it spread up to his cheeks and then his forehead. "So it's like that?"

The doctor spread his hands. "I'm sorry, but I have to ask."

"We were engaged. I don't have to prove it to you."

"No, you don't. But I would like something."

"What about him?" Arbeddo said and shoved the papers at me; they whiffled and fluttered, a noisemaker at a party gone quiet. "You ask him to prove it?"

"Prove what?"

"Anything."

"He brought her in. I think that proves something," said Macintyre.

"What?"

The doctor looked at him and nodded. "Maybe you're right." He put out his hand for the papers, and Joe Arbeddo put them in the doctor's open hand.

"You can have 'em," Joe said. "Go wipe your ass with 'em." He whipped around, strode down the corridor, and slammed the exit bar on the door, shoving it against its stops. The hard staccato of his boot heels went with him.

"Well," said Macintyre.

"Yeah," I said.

"I guess I better go to legal on this. It's looking tangled."

"It's probably best."

"I seem to spend as much time talking to lawyers and accountants as patients these days."

"We're the scum of the earth," I said.

"I didn't mean you. I just meant . . ."

"Don't worry about it," I said, waving a hand. I turned to go. "Can I call for an update?"

"Give me your card. I'll call you with the test results. I will have talked to legal by then."

I stopped and handed him a card from my wallet, and his eyebrows went up when he read it.

"I thought you were a lawyer."

"Nope. Lowly accountant."

"Taxes?"

"Taxes, estate planning." I looked back at Christina's room and took a very deep breath.

"I'll call you," he said. Then he turned and went down the hall and disappeared into another numbered room, continuing his rounds.

Chapter 15

The fresh air outside seemed as pure as oxygen straight from a cylinder. The stink of disinfectant, nitrile gloves, and the metallic smell of blood and bodily fluids had settled on my clothes and hair. As I walked down the broad sidewalk, looking up at the massive cliffs of Parnassus Heights behind the hospital building, I finally felt a breeze come up from the Cole Valley off Stanyan Street. Beyond, Stow Lake nestled like a sapphire pendant waiting for the skulking fog to steal its jeweled light.

I had arrived in the back of Christina's ambulance, and taxis were a rare sight around the hospital complex. I pulled my eyes off the lake and began the walk down the hill toward Stanyan to look for a taxi stand. Failing that, I would have to call and get on the rush hour queue so that a rude dispatcher could lie to me about how soon a dial cab would meet me.

Wind began to brush away the decaying smells and gray memory that had settled over me. A dark Chevy Caprice without hubcaps pulled to the curb and idled at my side. The dark glass of the driver's door rolled down, and DA Guthrie poked his square face and stubbled head out.

"Mr. Smoller, I presume," he said.

"I'm not in the mood, Guthrie," I said and kept walking. The car kept rolling. I hoped if I kept it up for half a block he might rear-end a parked minivan ahead. I could be a witness for the prosecution and attest to his driving negligence and get his license revoked. And pretty soon he'd bring me some good news, too.

He moved the car into the curb ahead of me and opened the door. He put a loafered foot on the pavement. The open door panel was blocking my way, but there was plenty of room to go around it. As I got nearer I could see his blue eyes, a shade so vibrant you could feel the energy and light vibrate in them. I slowed to get a better look inside and saw he was alone; I stopped. I rested my right arm on the door.

"Max," he said, "I thought we were friends."

"Right," I said. "I love talking to you right when all my old friends are dead or dying."

He looked up from my arm, taking ownership of his door, and met my eyes. "I'm sorry about that. The doctor says he'll have tests ready later in the day."

"Did you already talk to him? Before me?"

He shrugged. Up ahead a van started to crawl through hospital traffic. It was beaten-up and holed with rust, but it had the disc of an old-time loudspeaker welded flimsily to a roof rack. It was making noise, though I couldn't hear words or melody, and the wind ripping behind me carried the noise out toward the fog belt encroaching over the bastion of sun in the valley. The lake water was beginning to froth with whitecaps, angry at the approaching extinguishment of light. Behind the van I could see people walking and holding signs.

Guthrie put one hand on the front windowsill and the other on the door pillar. He pulled himself out of the car and stood up. My arm came off the top of the window and we turned into the sidewalk.

"We got the autopsy results," he said. His words slapped harder than the biting wind.

"I thought you said . . ."

"I said he'd been killed with his baseball bat."

"And he'd been killed asleep."

"I only implied he'd been asleep," he said. "There were far more broken bones, mainly in his fingers. One elbow was shattered. There was blood under his fingernails." He poked at the ground with a tip of his shiny shoes. A lace had come untied. We watched it flop back and forth on the sidewalk.

"Gee, thanks for breaking it to me delicately," I said. "And the autopsy means what?"

"That he was awake."

"That he fought?"

"Oh, he fought. He fought like a cornered beast."

He bent down to the ground and gathered his laces. I could see his naked head beneath me. The blanket of darkness that I had evaded in the hospital covered me now, wrapped me in a confusion I couldn't unravel, a suffocating straitjacket. And now, underneath the confusion burbled a deep, curdling blood anger. I used it to get a grip on myself.

"What the hell does this have to do with me?"

Guthrie looked up from his laces on the sidewalk and his fingers stilled. "Wouldn't you rather he went out fighting? Than get smacked in his sleep?"

"Does it matter?"

"I think the way you die does, yes."

"He was no hero."

"Nobody is. But it seems better that way to me."

"What are you telling me?"

"Just what I told you."

"No, there's something more."

He bent over his shoelaces and whipped them into a knot. The folds of skin on his neck bunched up under the collar.

"He knew," I said.

Guthrie finished and tugged hard at the loops. He got up, sucking in a deep breath.

"Yes. He knew his attacker."

"And this is your great evidence against Christina? That he knew her? That'll really shock a jury."

"Actually it cuts the other way."

"Pardon?"

"I said it cuts the other way."

"Really?"

"Yes. Really."

"How so?"

Guthrie took my shoulder and turned me into the lee of the building. The van and loudspeaker were closer now, and behind them were fifty or sixty assorted people holding signs. Some said, NO TO BUSH'S WAR; one said, WE ARE THE TERRORISTS. The metallic voice blasting out of the loudspeaker was more conversational. It wanted me to call my congressman, write my senator, stop paying taxes. Guthrie pulled me farther into the recesses and marble pillars of the outdoor lobby that guarded one of the medical office buildings. His hold on my attention was stronger than the commotion in the street.

"It cuts the other way because she's a small woman," he said. "I know some defense attorney will create doubt in a jury just from that. Joe was six one, two fifty. Christina's what? One twenty?"

"One ten. Maybe even ninety now," I said, and looked right into his face. He had the conscience to nod.

"The ME said the bones in the hands and elbow were broken before death."

"They can tell that closely? In time, I mean?"

"They think they can. Of course, nobody knows for sure. It's opinion dressed up as science. But it's a knowledgeable judgment. He's seen thousands before. Anyway, the clincher is the fingernails."

"They were broken?"

"It's unlikely they were anything but reflex wounds or conflict fractures."

"Those are what they sound like?"

"Yes. Sanitized, but yes."

"So Joe put up his hands."

"That's the reflex part."

"The killer broke them along with the nails."

"Yes."

"And I thought what I do for a living was ugly sometimes."

He turned me back out toward the street, which was emptying now while a black-and-white, its Christmas tree flashing, trailed after the protesters as they descended another hill and went down out of earshot.

"I hear you've been talking to Hopkins and Hannaford," he said.

"More like they've been talking to me."

"Maybe."

"You think I can make them do what I please?"

"No," he said, sliding his hands in his pockets. Then, "I'm going to tell the chief to give them some running room."

"Christina's no longer a suspect?"

"I didn't say that. She's still the only one with motive."

"You're stretching."

"No. You know that money is always the best trail."

"Cash leaves no trail," I said.

"It always gets you in the end. The money," he said. "As certain as hell."

"Or death and taxes," I said. I know a lot about the second and was learning much too fast about the first.

Chapter 16

I always worry when I get lucky. So I wasn't overjoyed when I got down Parnassus Heights to Stanyan, where an elderly lady shrugged out of a red-and-white dial cab. It didn't stop me from getting in the back before the door shut or air had filled the seat cushions back up. The Cab Fairy, quite distinct from the Parking Fairy and requiring far different prayers, offerings, sacrifices, and supplications, had smiled upon me. And I was suspicious, for I had not prayed.

The cabbie was an Afghan living in Fremont across the bay, having brought his growing collection of Pashtun family there for ten years. He had on a black skullcap from which black curls escaped down his neck and over his leathery skin. Next to his medallion number on the license was his name: Mirador Afshani. He owned the cab. When I asked him how he had bought it, he smiled a yellow smile out of his dark beard. "My wife is very . . .

certain woman, she likes things certain way?" he said. "But she is very good cook."

"Most women are certain," I said.

"Especially about cab. She say I must own, so I work construction, building, bad jobs, driving at city morgue."

"You drove the morgue wagon?"

"Yes, they call it this. How do you know?" he said, studying me at length in his rearview mirror.

I shrugged, and he finished, saying, "Anyway, she makes me buy cab."

I toyed with the thought of going home and at least getting back to the office where Irene could nag me back to normality, but I knew I had to talk to H & H. In my mind I had begun calling them that. So I told Afshani to take me to the precinct, and he turned the cab downhill.

The Park House Police Station, a squat redbrick building with nineteenth-century eaves and twenty-first-century dirt, was just off Stanyan. I could have walked, but I didn't feel like traipsing through the quaint dilapidation of Haight-Ashbury and seeing the flower children's grandchildren selling T-shirts, coffee mugs, porn videos, or bootleg cigarettes next to national retail chains. Afshani did not object to the quick drop-off. I tipped well and walked up the station house's smooth brick steps.

The desk sergeant culled both my driver's license and credit card, ran them through a computer check, and passed me through a metal detector before I was released to wander back to the homicide desk. H & H's cubicle had a view of the park, where Kezar Stadium squatted on Martin Luther King Drive as it snaked around and intersected with the Golden Gate Park's other twin artery, JFK Drive. MLK and JFK: the two were forever entwined in the park and the city's pantheon. H & H didn't seem surprised to see me.

"Hey," they said. "Guthrie called."

"Ah."

"We got a few extra days from the chief."

"That's good."

"Probably won't be enough."

"Why not?"

"Nothing obvious from the autopsy. No easy collar. We need more than a few more days."

"Guthrie said they learned a lot from the autopsy."

"Sure we did. Just not what we were hoping."

"Which was?"

"We wanted some DNA. Some skin under the nails, some hair, something that we could wrap up with motive, follow it back, and then ID the murderer."

"I see."

"So a few more days may not be enough."

"I see."

"We're not giving up."

"I know."

"We'll keep you posted."

"Hope so."

I turned to go. The light from the park streamed into the cubicle. Kezar Stadium was empty, the vacant seats standing like so many open palms begging to be filled.

"Listen," Arty said, "Guthrie talked to the doc just after you left."

I turned around and sat down in the wire chair in the middle of their joint office space.

"It's a tumor, like he thought."

I had thought I was prepared for that. Macintyre had said it. But the weight of it, the certainty of it, fell on my chest like heavy stones.

Chapter 17

The IRS's Northern California division office was, strangely, not in San Francisco. That offended transplanted natives like me who thought the city was the center of all intelligent life. Senior Agent Armand Redfield's branch office was in Oakland, the hinterlands.

I crossed the first leg of the Bay Bridge, flashing by Treasure Island, then past the huge storklike arms of the loading dock cranes on the Oakland wharfs off to the south. I negotiated the confusion of signs, turnoffs, exits, and traffic racing across lanes to 880 East or 580 West, blocks of dilapidated, sagging warehouses, fading advertisements from the '40s and '50s, until finally I was dumped by the exit overpass on Oakland's downtown streets.

As I passed the barren marquees of old theaters and new For

Lease signs on vacant department stores, I began to appreciate why the IRS had located here: rents a third of the price of downtown San Francisco, with cheap housing close by. GS-2s and GS-3s could even commute through the Altamont gap of the Oakland Hills. There the Central Valley bulged virally on the other side, and cheaper bedroom communities were springing up like dandelions on new turf grass. It was practically the only place people earning less than fifty grand a year could live in the Bay Area.

At the end of Main Street in Oakland, after two car dealerships, a medical clinic, and a Blimpie, street people loitered with assorted cardboard boxes or shopping carts. Next door a squat four-story office building planted itself firmly on the corner of Main and Twenty-Third. A band of reflective glass windows and cantilevers of cement on each floor striated it horizontally. I walked through the plate-glass entryway and up to Armand's office, listed under IRS District Field Office in a black-and-white-lettered directory.

I felt a flutter of nerves tickle at my arm and right hand as I reached for the stainless steel doorknob to the field office. The receptionist, a GS-3, sat at the ready. I heard my mind click *GS-3, GS-3* in uncontrolled idiocy. Her plump face smiled up at me in practiced courtesy, and I watched the V of her hefty décolletage twist as she turned to an expensive keyboard.

"Ms. Marsapo is not available; would you like voice mail?" She tapped a button, daintily popping her fingers on the appropriate extension as she turned back to me. As she tilted her eyes up I saw iridescent green rounded out by deep black irises. She would have been stunning without the disguise of an extra hundred pounds. I found myself pitying her, imagining marathons on the couch watching reality TV, guzzling diet soda, and eating pizza.

"Can I help you?" she asked, a vertical furrow digging at the bridge of her nose, darting upward to her broad forehead.

"Armand Redfield, please."

"An appointment?" she asked and put a hand on the desk. I saw the blue back of a tattoo in the web between thumb and forefinger. The mark of a Buddhist meditator. Even in a GS-3. First Hannaford, now Armand's receptionist.

"Yes. He's expecting me."

The receptionist pointed me down the hall, my mind screeching *GS-3, GS-3*, a howler monkey on steroids. Inside an office with a door open to the hall, Redfield was sitting behind an expansive desk of dark wood—walnut or stained cherry—with a series of files piled in intermittent mesas on the desktop. He stood up, and his lean frame was silhouetted by the large window in back of him. Through the window the land arched up steep hillsides into the Berkeley Hills. On the sill I counted three old coffee mugs with the string flags of tea bags hanging off their handles. *A tea man*, I thought. Strange I didn't remember.

Redfield walked around the desk as I approached. His face was kinked with lines of age that had not been there years before and that I had not noticed in the hospitable light at Joe's house. The furrows on his cheeks were deep and well worn. In through the open window, the bright day smells of dry earth and black oak from the hillside wafted in. He stopped at one desk corner and motioned with an open palm to an armchair, modern steel and black leather.

"Nice of you to come slumming, Max." The East Bay shoulder chip was reflexive, and he smiled through it.

"No problem, Armand. I wanted to ask you something at Joe's wake, but you vanished just when I was going to talk to you about it."

"What is it?"

"It's about Joe. And Kessler. What did you want with him?"

"I told you. Pure curiosity. In my world he's a celeb, a billionaire. So is Stoppard. How many times is a GS-10 going to get to rub elbows with high rollers like that?"

"So you just wanted to come home and gossip about George Stoppard?"

"It's better than listening to my wife read *People* magazine out loud at dinner."

He smiled and sat down on a corner of the desk. I looked up at him. His face stayed friendly. Joe might have been right: somebody had to be on the take in the audit chain, but Armand had always had a flair of disgust for wealthy tax dodgers. He loved nothing better than making a three-piece, four-thousand-dollar suit do a perp walk with cameras blazing and newspaper ink flowing.

"How is Carol?" I asked. His wife had been the pie and cookies type, a sweetheart straight from a high school yearbook.

"Kids are fine. College. Scholarships. We're set. When I hit my twenty, I'm outta here."

"You should have a pretty nice pension by now."

"Only good thing about being a GS-10. You know that."

I stuck out my feet and struggled out of the chair. Its angled seat made getting out of it a two-armed affair.

"I talked with Joe before he died."

"Why?" he asked.

A strange question. No when, no what about, no surprise. Outside, a couple of jays squawked, flying tight figure eights up and down, then landing on an oak.

He said, "I mean, I heard you and Joe weren't close since . . ."

"Since Christina, you mean?" I asked, standing now, aching to take a stab at him and make him stand, too.

"Sure, I mean, don't get me wrong. I never saw the attraction; Christina was a little transparent for me."

"You knew her well, did you?"

"No. But before you left . . ."

"Fired. You fired me."

"You were never going to be able to follow orders and deal with the bureaucracy. I did you a favor."

"Maybe. I talked to the police and the DA. Joe was under the heat. They were looking for someone doing fraudulent shelters. But then he . . . they found Christina, and no one wants to look further than the obvious. Joe thought there was something, someone gone bad in the audit."

"Joe loved conspiracy. You know that. Sometimes, often, the obvious is true. We see that all the time. So must you."

"Christina beat Joe's head in with a baseball bat? She's got a tumor bigger than a baseball in her head. And she's weaker than a kitten."

"Too bad you're not the DA. Your lady love would be free as a bird."

"Listen, Armand, Joe told me someone in the Service was taking bribes."

"Really."

"Any idea who that might be?" I asked.

"Oh, yeah. It's me. I confess." He came off the desk. "Get out of here, Max, before I tell Guthrie he ought to look at you. I want anyone who's taking kickbacks a whole lot more than I want Joe's killer."

"That a fact?"

"That's right. And I'd watch your back if I were you. Joe's clients almost always know each other. And a lot of them are your clients. Across the bay it's still a pretty small town, when you put together a hundred key people."

"The reputation-is-everything speech, Armand? That it?"

"Something like it."

I tasted bile in the back of my throat and choked down his obvious threat. I forced a grin onto my face. It felt like breaking plaster.

"Nice talking to you, Armand. You better get your pension soon, because you've been doing the IRS sheriff speech too long. It just doesn't hold together anymore."

I turned and walked away from him toward the paneled door. I waited for a comeback reply, but none came, and as I went through the door his back was turned. One of the mugs from the windowsill was in his hand as he faced the green and tawny walls of the mountains behind us.

Chapter 18

After I left Armand, I drove back across the Bay Bridge. The city rose ahead of me in sunny splendor, a noonday sky whisked clean of clouds by a blustery spring wind scouring the bridge's steel past the avenues and into downtown.

I drove into this headwind, deflated and unsure of myself. Armand had always been someone I despised, even hated, especially when he terminated me for what was really insubordination.

I had refused to threaten some poor cab owner in the city with jail time and instead told him to file a couple of extensions and get a tax lawyer. Armand had found out because it was the third or fourth time one of these small fry had bailed on us. I just couldn't get excited when some guy was working seventy hours a week and taking out an extra fifty thousand a year in mad money the government couldn't get.

There were developers' finance guys, Internet darlings, or hedge fund honchos pulling down two million, three million, four million a year in salary, ten times that in cap gains or profits. I had wanted to go after capital gains treatment of profits on hedge funds. That we could audit. But Armand showed me the numbers, how it was too expensive to chase them behind their Belize holding companies and tax shelters with offshore accounts and high-priced lawyers. We couldn't afford to audit, much less litigate. So we went after the small fry.

I quit. Or got terminated, downsized, fired, or whatever you want to label it. So I started my own practice doing small-fry returns, expecting a small-fry life until Joe started making recommendations to his clients to see me. And he gave me the fund's tax returns to do. Easy, but a good selling point.

And now I had ended up doing tax shelters for the guys I had wanted to audit all those years ago.

I was supposed to feel guilty. I was supposed to think I had sold out. But I didn't. I had made my peace with the world. I could have tilted at the windmills of my reality, but nobody did that anymore. The big money printed the bills and ran the regulatory boards, the development commissions appointed by the governor, the financial accounting standards board, the SEC, the World Bank. Everything. The system was impregnable, from shop owner to factory worker carrying slogans for God, country, and no gay marriage.

It was their world now, and I was just going to walk through it.

I got past the bridge traffic and off the exit into the pedestrian snarl of downtown. A vague bile of nausea barbed at my throat as I waited impatiently for the lights to turn so I could crawl through lunchtime crosswalkers who knew that, according to California law, they had the right of way on city streets.

Finally I broke through at the Transamerica tower to freedom on Broadway and turned right on Filbert to climb the back of Telegraph Hill. I parked, looking forward to my office oasis where I could stare out at the bay. Work was piling up in advance of April 15, and I had thirty days to finish the returns many of my clients had already sent me. Their collections of jam-spotted receipts or coffee-stained deductions waited in binders on my desk.

I parked in the garage on Filbert that cost me $500 a month and was dark and dank, sinking into the hill, then climbed the piss-filled stairs to sunlight. Hiked the tilted street to the corner of Montgomery, past the little corner deli that subsisted on low rent and homeowners unwilling to go down Telegraph Hill for milk or cigarettes.

My hands were dying for a cigarette, as were my lungs. And just as I walked into the tree-lined quiet and approached my redoubt of safety, I saw Irene outside pacing, and of all things, smoking. She had never smoked. Not ever. Not once.

I walked closer. She glared my way and immediately threw her cigarette to the ground. Then she began to clomp back toward our front door.

"Irene," I called after her. She kept walking, a flare to the hem of her dress as she speeded up, held back from running by her wooden clogs.

"Irene, wait." Something in my voice stopped her and she stood ramrod straight, still with her back to me. I jogged a few steps and caught up to her. As I walked close, I put a hand on her upper arm to turn her around. She shrugged it off with a jerk of her shoulder. Her head was bowed as I walked around her, and I could see wet eyelashes on her down-turned cheeks.

"Irene, what's the matter?"

She kept her head down, her bright lashes flashing, sunlight on dewdrops.

"Nothing." She shook her head as teardrops whisked off her eyes like water from a shaking dog.

"Nothing? Doesn't look like nothing. Tell me what's wrong. Is your uncle okay?"

She took a deep breath and shook her head in a way I didn't like, looking away from me, something in her expression, some insult, some disappointment, some truth. She waved her hand at the office.

"Danny Cleveland's in there."

"So? Why? What's he doing here?"

Finally she turned around, her eyes still moist but her head up, chest out, heart free. I could see it, beating as if she had no skin. Pride showing through her tears and the effort of getting her face together.

"Those are a lot of questions, Max. Which one do you want me to answer?"

"The one about why you're crying."

Irene looked at me with tears falling from angry eyes.

"He's a nasty guy. And he has some bad news."

"So he wants his five grand back. I did strike out with Redfield."

"He says he's chairman of Amagansett. Joe's hedge fund? They're pulling their accounts."

"That was gonna happen anyway, Irene. It's no big deal."

"The Stoppard Trust pulled its account too." That was a problem. A big problem. My biggest account.

"How did he know that?"

"Says he's on the board as a consultant or something. He was pretty vague."

"What did he tell you?"

"Nothing."

"How could it be nothing if it upset you?"

"I realized it was just . . . a fucking waste of time. We're off. Done."

"I've never heard you swear."

"I'm learning," she said.

"What did he say?"

"Just gossip."

"Irene."

"All right," she said, finally looking up at me, "you asked." And here she took a deep breath in her lungs. "He said you had been screwing around with Christina again. Recently. After the funeral."

"He said that?"

"He did."

"I'll rip his fucking head off. That little shit."

"Is it true?"

"No! For God's sake, Irene. Is that what you're upset about? You should know me better than that. I should be insulted. How can you doubt my integrity like that?"

"It was important to me."

"It's important to me, too, Irene."

"To know the guy . . . the man I work for is honest. You know that matters."

"Well, the guy you work for is about to beat up a cripple," I said, and stormed for my front door. "Watch this," I said.

"Watch out," she said. As usual she was right.

When I walked in, Danny Cleveland's right plastic hand was lying on the table. He was not attached to it and was drinking a glass of water from a pitcher full of ice on the credenza. The hand lay on the table, a practical joke, a plastic tarantula, fat and heavy on a pillow. The fingers were bent and curled, ready to crawl away in movement. I looked at it a little closer. It wasn't the same color, that plastic of human tan and peeling neoprene polish. There were no attachments, but two small empty buckles hung off each side of the upper wrist.

He saw me looking at it. He saw my face. I could feel his anger bottle up as I looked at the hand in the center of the table. He poked his chin at the dead, spidery hand.

"My real one's in the shop. This one's just a strap on. Pretty worthless. Can barely hold change with it. It's a hell of a club though. I don't think I'll be having trouble with the Gaslight Boys."

"Gaslight Boys?"

"The rough kids. Short pants. Underwear showing. Think they're hard. We call them Gaslight Boys back home."

"You're from Ireland?"

"My grandparents."

"Why don't you can the Danny Boy act then?"

"That's a lot of hostility you've got building there, Mr. Smoller."

"What are you doing here? What did you say to Irene?"

"Only the truth, dear boy, only the truth."

"What's that?"

"I'm chairman of Amagansett. Did Joe tell you?"

"No."

"You can check with the funds' lawyers. Anyway . . ."

"What have you got to do with the Stoppard Trust?"

"They're a limited partner in Amagansett. At George Stoppard's persuasion, of course."

"So you know George, too?"

"Of course, my boy. So did Joe."

"You have the authority to change their accountants?" I demanded.

"These things never work that way. A little chat over a beer on the tenth hole. A few peanuts on the eighteenth. Some discreet conversation, and the next time your engagement runs out." He shrugged. "At tax time, every year, dear boy. It's over. On to a big firm. There really is no reason to go with a small fry like you."

"What did you tell Irene about Christina?"

"Just that you'd been at her hotel the other night. Right before the funeral."

"You tell her I slept with her?"

"Did you?" he asked. Before I could answer, he held up his hand. "Wonderful gossip, you know. Whiff of scandal. Might even make the society pages of the *Chronicle*. Another Dede Wilsey story, but with a murder. How could an editor resist?"

"Why don't you tell me why you're here? Why didn't you tell me you were on the board of Joe's funds? For that matter, why didn't Joe tell me?"

"I'm sure he felt it was an unnecessary complication. I just wanted some help with my tax refund."

He went over to the table and picked up his hand. The wrist stuck out. Then he pulled out two leather straps from his right sleeve. He threaded the straps through the buckles and bent his head to grasp one leather strap with his teeth. He pulled tight on one, then the other. His right hand stuck out of his sleeve. He pulled his jacket down over the wrist.

"It becomes itchy when I sweat." He shrugged. "I walked up the Filbert Steps from down on Sansome. A huge mistake. Must be three hundred steps."

"Four hundred seventy-nine," I said, having climbed it many times.

"I came for a reason, Max. A good reason. I'm on your side, though you may not know it. So, please, do as George asks. He's much more involved in your affairs than you thought. Joe saw to that."

"I didn't know George was that involved in the trusts."

"But I'm here to tell you. There's nothing to this idea of Joe's. There was no bribing of officials. People like Kessler and Stoppard don't do that. They don't need to do that. They have enough already. How could you think they were so stupid?"

"I don't think they're stupid. I just don't know whether they pay their taxes."

"Joe was a little nuts at the end. His funds were going south. He was worried about raising money. People were about to flee. Returns were going negative. Believe me."

"Did he have redemptions?"

"Not yet," Danny said, "not yet. But I am not here to talk about Joe or even Amagansett. I'm here to tell you I've decided to go ahead and take my refund. Keep that money I gave you. I know you tried with Armand."

"Why are you keeping the refund? How do you know I talked to Armand?"

"Joe told me to hire you. He thought Redfield would never meet with him."

"Did you have me followed?"

"Joe wanted to get you and Armand together. He didn't think he should try with Armand."

"He was right. If Armand met with him and it came out, he'd lose everything."

"That's why he asked me to make up this refund story."

"It was the damnedest thing I ever heard. Still is."

"Well, it got you talking to Armand. He saw you, didn't he?"

"The IRS talks to accountants all the time."

"Exactly."

"So you cooked up the refund to do what?"

"Joe was sure Armand was behind his audits. Especially when Armand tried to go back three years."

"That's why he said he brought me in," I said. "Those were my returns."

"Exactly. So you see. He had to call you."

"Look. I want you out of my life right now. Get out."

"All right, my boy, I'll go. But you'll still need to go after Armand."

"Why?"

"Because he's looking at those three back years."

"I did them myself."

"That's why Joe asked me to talk to you, remember?"

"He won't find anything."

"Joe was counting on it."

Danny put his right hand back in his jacket pocket and pulled away from the table he'd been leaning on. He walked past me, his sallow face flashing as he went by. That flash picture that your mind takes that won't go away. It stayed with me as I heard him go down the stairs.

Joe was counting on it. Joe was counting on it. To put me between him and the feds? What if . . . What if he really had done something wrong? What if there really was fraud? What if those shelters were designed for maximum benefit and were way past the edge of the code?

I could have always fallen back on Joe, given the old defense: I just did what my client's records showed. No liability here, Armand. No crime in that. Maybe a little stupid. But Joe was my friend. I didn't think he'd do anything like that.

But Joe was gone and there wasn't anything between me and Armand now.

Chapter 19

On that morning I was wrapped in fog. I had woken well before dawn and launched myself showered but unshaven out into wet and shrouded streets. The car was damp and cold. My hands on the wheel retracted from the touch of chilled, clammy leather, and my heater took precious minutes to warm the seats.

I drove up the back of Telegraph Hill. The stop signs were glazed with dew and the streetlights haloed with a weak sun circled by clouds presaging rain. I parked down the street from my office, climbed the steps, and luxuriated in the heat from the radiators I had installed throughout the old building. The coffee urn had already fired off, set at 5 a.m. for just these types of early mornings or sleepless nights. I took a fresh cup out of the thermal carafe and sat down at my desk to stare out over the invisible bay wrapped in its cocoon.

I worked on some returns but with no concentration or attention. Danny Cleveland's case was done, if only because, whatever he was trying to pull, he kept the refund; a victory in these instances. Just one more example of how guys like Cleveland and Kessler win even when they lose.

I knew as I went through them, checking that credit boxes were filled in properly and the numbers footed, that these were my last cases. I had not done this work since the early days of my practice and had since farmed it out to an eager young accountant, Mario Pantella, who did fast and excellent work, freeing me from worry and embarrassment from my clients.

But now I was doing it myself, a bittersweet ache in my hands and chest as I looked into the morning mist. My last return, my last 1040. *I can't really believe you're going to do this, put up and quit and jump into what?* And the answer came. *Something more important than this.*

Then a knock sounded on the door. The knocking stopped, then started again as I remained in my chair, not wanting to walk down three flights of stairs. It was before seven and Irene didn't arrive until eight. Finally, as the pounding threatened the door's joints, I walked downstairs.

I yanked the door open. Standing in the fog, both of their collars turned up against the chill morning wind, were Napoleon and Arty.

They stood on the steps, two blackened beasts of prey, heavy with portent.

"We need your coffee," the portent said.

I turned around from them and didn't close the door. They followed me into the entry hall and down the shining blond wood floor and into our kitchen where the thermal carafe rested like a prize on an altar. Arty went straight to a cabinet and got some buffalo china mugs. Napoleon pulled metal chairs up to the small breakfast table.

Arty poured black oily coffee into the mugs, and steam rose from them. The bitter smell filled the air. I could feel warmth through the mug in my hands. No one spoke. The clinking noise of the spoons stirring sugar into cups, plops of milk competed with the hum of the fridge. We hunkered down, taking small sips until the caffeine hit us and chased the remnants of sleep away. That first sip in the morning, food for the famished, speed for the weary, sunlight for the blue.

"So, Max," Nappy finally said, pushing his coffee away from him and straightening up, "we got some news."

"Some bad news," Arty said, stabbing a glance at his partner.

"Christina? She's dead?" I asked. I knew her tumor had grown.

"Went over to the DA yesterday," he said, like *yest-ta-dee*, like my mom's old friends from up near Boston, "and Guthrie laid out the case for us."

"It's pretty tight," Napoleon said.

"Compelling," Arty added.

I pushed my coffee away.

"Great. Hurray for you. Go on home now. Case closed," I said.

"C'mon, Max. We tried. You know that."

"You did your duty, okay?" I said to the two of them. They leaned backward, looked down at their coffee, and put the mugs on the table. I could see in their calm and blank faces that they had expected this. They were sitting there letting my anger wash over them. I had known this had to come, but I had to do it just the same.

"Go on home. You told me," I said, weary now, very suddenly weary, with no anger to fuel my exhaustion. I needed more coffee so I got some and chugged it after a huge dollop of milk cooled it down. It still tasted bitter, the glory of that first cup gone. I was angry at it being gone, just as I was when the sun rises into noon and morning happiness goes with it. I just had these two friends, new friends that felt like old ones because of what we'd been through. They were watching me the way old friends do when they're worried. Worried and they have bad news.

Chapter 20

By afternoon, heat finally cleared the streets of fog, if only briefly. Shiny cars glinted in the mounting morning sun. There was no traffic on California Street as my Audi climbed Nob Hill, and the trolleys slid by nearly empty in the dandelion morning light. I dawdled at the top, puttered on slowly to Divisadero, letting two cars go through the stop signs before I accelerated through.

Joe's house loomed large against the sky as I came up the last incline to the top of the Heights. That last humpback gave the pillared mansions there three-sixty-degree views of diamond-sparkled ocean, placid bay, and tan building-studded cityscape, worth every penny now. There was a white van in the driveway and a Honda parked out front when I got there, but otherwise the house was shuttered and drawn.

I walked up those long, wide steps I had climbed so long ago, three ancient weeks ago.

I felt strangely shorn of volition; my feet strode up the steps with energy I did not possess, and my hand punched the doorbell and grasped the knob with a determination not mine. The white door opened with my touch, and standing behind it was a black-haired man in nurse's whites with a prizefighter's nose and broad Mestizo cheekbones. He looked over his shoulder and then turned aside to let me in. Behind him was Guthrie. He had his hat in his hand again, just as when we had met that first day, that unforgotten day, in Joe's office. He nodded at the man dressed in white, who swiveled, the rubber soles of his scuffed leather shoes squeaking on the white marble squares. They were strange shoes for a male nurse, I thought.

Guthrie moved forward. He slowly rotated the brim of the hat through his fingers like a wheel. He waited before he spoke, looking past me at the ceiling.

"You don't seem surprised to see me," he said at last. And I realized I wasn't. I shook my head. He continued. "You can see her. I think I've asked as much as I needed to."

I was about to ask him what they talked about and what he was going to do with her, but I hesitated, trying to think how to phrase it so I wouldn't presume or telegraph innocence or guilt to him. But before I made up my mind or opened my mouth he had started for the door. I didn't move a muscle until the front door clicked shut behind me.

I walked down the hallway into the connected den. It had been Joe's office once, three long-gone weeks ago. Someone had converted it into a bedroom, since it was on the ground floor and had a private full bath. It saved the nurses from carrying food and supplies up and down stairs all day, though it seemed odd, unlike Christina to sacrifice her view and comfort for that of the staff.

At the end of the hall, carpeted and quiet underfoot, I rapped a knuckle on the door and heard her say "Come in." Through the door her voice sounded high-pitched and birdlike, warbling through quick octaves.

I opened the door on her sitting in a pink bathrobe, a waxen face and dark smudged eyes above it. She was propped up against a satin-covered headrest. She pointed an open hand around the room, to the marred view over the bay, out to the deep beyond the bridge, blocked by the trees and hedges of the grounds.

"Like my view now?" she said. I smiled and nodded as if I meant it, and she smiled and nodded as if she thought I did.

"It looked better than the one upstairs," she explained. And slow as always, I got it. There had been the stain on the bedroom rug upstairs, still amoeba-like and present.

"I tried new rugs," she confirmed. I could only nod and paint a lopsided smile on my face. She had only one place to live now, the house Joe had been killed in, and not long to live there, either.

I nodded at the carpets underneath her bed. "They look new," I said. I thought of the room upstairs and Joe crying for life as someone crushed his head with a Louisville Slugger. My stomach twisted into a knot. Acidic sadness crept up and burned my throat, and I felt its force and pressure behind my eyes.

"I meant upstairs, moron." She smiled, her lopsided face breaking into something more natural, close to real.

"Sorry. Really sorry," I said.

She waved at me and looked out the windowpane. I could see her Adam's apple bob up and down in a swallow where her neck was silhouetted against the brightness of the window and the green of the trees outside. Her neck was thin and swan white. I sat down on a green-brocaded club chair, the only color in that room with the white hospital bed and the IV pole and the drab and silent monitoring equipment. The color was the Kelly green she had loved.

"You talk to my doctors?" she asked, turning her head, with its short, stubby hair, back toward me.

"They wouldn't tell me anything if I asked, unless you authorized them. But I talked to H & H."

"H & H?"

"Sorry. That's what I call Napoleon and Arty. Hopkins and Hannaford. H & H."

"Like the Green Stamps." She smiled.

"Like that," I said. "They told me."

"I guess drama like this doesn't stay quiet for long."

"I guess not," I said.

"My doctor said he could go in . . ." She looked out the window again, and I saw her Adam's apple bob once, twice, outlined against the windowpane. It was bony and stuck out, the skin of the neck sagging around her throat. I could hear her breath rasp and see hesitation at swallowing.

"Tumor's in the prefrontal lobe this time. To cut it . . . it would be like a lobotomy. Small odds of success, since there are other small ones all over." She turned back. "But the good news is they can't be small for long. Those little suckers are runners. Run, run, run all day long. 'Fore long they're all grown up."

"I know. I mean, I didn't know. The details, I didn't. But I know," I said, swallowing. "I know you don't have long."

"Guthrie told you," she said, this time fixing me with eyes, those still-beautiful, silent, soul-breaking eyes, squeezing my heart and throat until I became a strange mixture of blood and tears. She fixed those eyes on me.

She said, "Guthrie told me they weren't going to press charges."

"He said that?"

"He did."

"Just now?"

"Before you came. Before you walked in. He was nice, at least he was trying to be. But he made it clear he thought they had enough to prosecute. He said . . . he said . . ." and she stopped again and smiled, her small little smile, the broken eyes.

"He said he wouldn't waste taxpayers' money 'cause I had a longer sentence to be served." She blew out a big breath at the end and took in a full chest of air. I could see a piece of tape on her neck stretch and then wrinkle again against the skin. "Pretty self-righteous, our man Guthrie," she said, exhaling.

It was my turn to breathe, but I could barely get it in. "What did you say?"

"What could I say? 'Thanks. See you later. It was a gas, Guthrie. A blast. Let's do it again sometime.'"

I was about to ask "Really?" when she added, "Don't worry, Max. It was just 'thanks.' The rest was my embroidery."

I could not look at her then, and if I could have looked at her, I would not have seen her through the sudden haze of tears. I heard a river roar next to my ear, moving fast and dark, white water ahead. How could she die? We had lost it before we ever had it. I lost her once, and now she's going again. In front of me this time.

And then I came to the placid end of the rapids where the water lay flat with white suds after the rocks. The question I could neither speak nor avoid, could not flee nor face, swelled in me as a river high with runoff. My face pointed down, as water, a tear maybe, dropped off my face and dripped onto the carpet. I could see it splash and plop on the rug. Plop. Plop. Slowly, slowly, my head came up of its own accord.

She watched me.

"You want to know, don't you?" she asked.

I nodded. I felt the skin on the back of my neck bunch and cord, the muscle cramping tight.

"Everybody wants to know," she said. "Everybody."

"For God's sake, tell me what happened."

"Why?" she said.

"It can't possibly matter now," I said.

"You think just 'cause I'm dying I don't care what people think about me? You try dying and see what you want to confess. You're not a priest anyhow," she said, her tired chest rising and falling from the effort as she grabbed at the metal arm on the bed. My head was heavy, and I hung it down again, defeated by the bitterness that was in her and would camp with her to the death. Beyond it, too. I saw the rounded, small wet spot where I had dripped before. The spot seemed smaller to me, as if I had returned as a man to my childhood bedroom, all things shrunken and cramped.

"Do you really want to know, Max?" she asked while my head was down.

I looked up then with urgency, hardness, a need that came from nowhere and everywhere and seized me like a lust. "Yes. I want to know. But most of all, I want to know that you do," I said, using the desire that had arrived unwanted.

"So you are a confessor after all." She smiled. She grabbed with two bony hands, two elderly spotted hands, at her white sheets and pulled herself more upright.

"I didn't tell him to do it," she said. "I swear to you, I didn't."

I leaned back in the big chair, and breath vacated my body in relief. I looked up at the ceiling. I could have flown to it.

"Thank God," I said.

"But I did it," she said. "I never asked him to, but I might as well have."

"What do you mean?"

"I gave him money. I told him Joe's schedule. I made plans with him for after the divorce. I—"

"Why?"

"Why? Because. Because Joe was leaving me. Because I hit menopause. Because I deserve better. Because. Because. Because. What do the reasons matter? I did it. I goaded that poor, stupid, vicious, simple barnyard rooster of a concrete mason into doing my bidding. I knew what I was doing every step of the way. Like I was born to it."

"Jesus Christ, why?" I said.

"Because I was fucking angry," she said. "That enough of an answer? Is that what you wanted? To know all this? Do you feel better knowing, Max? Are you a better man for it?"

My chest burned with sadness so sharp I wanted a knife to cleave it out, take a razor down my windpipe, hydrochloric down my throat, anything—anything to burn away this knowledge.

Then I dragged my face to look at her and her round bulbous eyes and the moist lips and the neck straining, the head forward and off the pillow. I said to that ravaged, devoured face, "No, I don't feel better. And no, I'm not a better man for it. But I am more of a man for knowing. Though I don't suppose you would understand."

She moved a waxy hand at me. "At this point who gives a fuck about understanding?"

I watched her fingers pluck at the hem of the sheet, then

smooth the fabric on the small logs of her legs under the sheet. And still I wanted to hide, so I said, "I don't understand. This was the tumor, right? You weren't diagnosed, but it must have been growing in there. I mean there are all these cases of people losing brain function and doing crazy stuff. Other stuff. That could be you. Right?"

"Who the fuck knows, Max? Who cares?" she asked, now pounding her legs. "Who the fuck cares? I'll be dead in six weeks. Why does it matter?"

"It matters to me!" The words came out of my throat like a defect, a great, black, roaring hell of sorrow, dark and twisted and numb.

"That's only because you loved me," she said.

And then anger arrived; a savior, a saintly protection, a separation, a distance. I watched the miles fly away between us, and I was suddenly standing upright and empty. I felt I was looking down at her from great Olympian mountains, and I was in the cool summer breeze of high mountain air. She was down there below, small and exhausted and wan. Her hand still plucked the hem of the sheet, the last green light of bitterness remaining like a twitch all the way down to her fingertips. I looked down at her with the peaceful emptiness that truth and freedom bring. I said to her, "Once. Once I loved you dearly."

She looked up at me as I turned to leave, a sheen of fear over her eyes, but accepting my retreat as she faced me, her chin still strong and jutting.

"And it was a long time ago," she said.

I went to the door. Grasped the brass knob. Before I could go, she had one last question: "Will I see you again?"

I held the brass, its coolness welcome in my hand, but I did not turn to her.

"I'll be back a few times," I said. "Before you go."

"That's nice, Max. You were always a very nice man."

"All the good it does me," I said.

She didn't stop me anymore. I went out. I don't recall the plush carpet down the long hall and out through the marble foyer. Where my shoes must have clicked loudly in the empty hall.

From out of nowhere, the man in white appeared, his shoes squishing and squeaking on the marble as I opened the front door, the brass knocker glinting into my eyes from the high, harsh morning sun. He nodded at me and closed the door on my heels. I went down the steps and into my car, into the clear and gleaming slow motion of moments we remember forever.

After that I saw her three more times. She had fallen into a coma soon after that visit. She lasted only a week.

When I spoke to the doctor and the coroner—who Guthrie had insisted examine the body for any drugs or assisted suicide— the doctor expressed some surprise at the size of the remaining tumors.

The last visit I had waited there, nodding when she spoke, watching her look out the window, and proffering bromides or platitudes when she asked me questions I could not answer. Which was almost any question. Every question.

I could barely speak, but I returned and waited out of some instinct, some wish to see death and watch how it took Christina and to see what it would have to say or do for me. But of course Death is silent and speaks only to those he has come for. And I simply stood witness as the cancer ate what little remained of Christina.

I have asked myself many times since how those events could

have come to pass and what I have learned from them. And, in fact, this tale was a misguided effort to explain them to myself. As always, the mystery of ourselves eludes us, a bank of fog always out of reach or that when entered, obscures our vision even more.

But I lived beyond Christina and Joe and buried them both and came away with something. I had always wanted to know the truth, or believed I had, and had constructed a life I thought was dedicated to learning and recording and transmitting truth in numbers. And all I learned was how much I flee from truth in people, from the dark in intimate souls and places, from the dark in myself. Our shadows mingle and flow into deltas of the mind, meld with the clean and deep blue oceans of our souls. And we cannot tell one from the other, because they are the same substance, the same element, the same ocean. That is us, that is who we are. And trying to parse it into truth or numbers or Letters of Administration is a fool's job.

So now I walk the hills of my San Francisco, up the steep, wide streets and down the narrow, grounded blocks of North Beach or past the palaces of Pacific Heights, a fool no longer.

Acknowledgments

It was a surprise to no one but me: No book is an island, complete unto itself.

There are always far too many people who play a part in bringing a book to market than can be thanked, if only because the mythic solitary author does not really exist except in the pages or scenes of bad books and movies. Thanks to Kyle Jennings, the first editor/publisher to believe in my work, who agreed to sign a three-book contract with me and pointed out that *GGR* should lead the way. To Jane Friedman at Open Road, who believed in this book before I did, and to Nicole Passage and Jennifer Pooley for their herculean editing. And to the solitary hours given me by the four wonderful women in my life: my wife, Suzanne, and our daughters, Casey, Maddy, and Charlotte.

Copyright © 2012 by Jim Kohlberg

Cover design by Andrea C. Uva

ISBN 978-1-4532-6202-3

Published in 2012 by Open Road Integrated Media
180 Varick Street
New York, NY 10014
www.openroadmedia.com

Videos, Archival Documents, and New Releases

Sign up for the Open Road Media newsletter and get news delivered straight to your inbox.

FOLLOW US:
@openroadmedia and
Facebook.com/OpenRoadMedia